St. Pierre Boyz 2

All is Fair in Love & War

Mz. Lady P & Mesha Mesh

St. Pierre Boyz 2

Copyright © 2017 by Mz. Lady P & Mesha Mesh

Table of Contents

Previously in St. Pierre Boyz: All is Fair in Love and War
.... 1

Chapter One..7

Chapter Two..15

Chapter Three 21

Chapter Four...27

Chapter Five..35

Chapter Six...43

Chapter Seven...53

Chapter Eight..61

Chapter Nine 71

Chapter Ten 79

Chapter Eleven..85

Chapter Twelve 91

Chapter Thirteen 99

Chapter Fourteen 111

Chapter Fifteen...115

Chapter Sixteen...123

Chapter Seventeen 131

Chapter Eighteen..141

Chapter Nineteen...145

Chapter Twenty 149

Chapter Twenty-One 153

Chapter Twenty-Two...163

Chapter Twenty-Three 169

Chapter Twenty-Four 179

Chapter Twenty-Five 191

Chapter Twenty-Six...203

Chapter Twenty-Seven 209

Previously in St. Pierre Boyz: All is Fair in Love and War

I sat in a dark ass room holding onto my son for dear life. I couldn't believe the chain of events that landed my ass here with June's stupid ass. He wanted me to cry and suffer, but I refused to. This supposedly dead ass nigga would never get another tear out of Leilani Brooks. I cried every day for this nigga, and all along, he was alive and well. The moment I find happiness and move on with my life, he wants to pop up and call himself taking me from Luxe.

Speaking of Luxe, my heart was aching behind his actions. I knew he was too good to be true. I should have known there was a motive behind him wanting to be here for my son and me. I should have followed my first mind and kept it moving, but I just didn't want to believe that I was a pawn in his game to kill June.

My girls and I should have steered clear of the infamous St. Pierre Boyz, because life had been one big ass rollercoaster ride for us since meeting them. I'm not gone front, though. Luxe has brought so much joy into my life I couldn't help but be hurt by his actions.

"Mama, I want to go home. Is Luxe coming to get us?" I quickly squeezed Juju tightly, because I didn't want June to whoop him again. When we first made it to this apartment that he's holding us in, Juju started falling all out and having a tantrum for Luxe, and June didn't like that shit one bit. I cried watching him whoop my son. After he was finishing whooping him, he turned around and beat my ass. I was trying to be strong, but he had been beating my ass from the moment he snatched me up.

"Didn't I tell you not to ask for that nigga again?" June was now holding Juju by his collar talking to him.

"Yes."

"Yes, what?"

"Yes, Daddy."

"Here. I have some games on my phone. I want you to go into the other room and play them. I need to talk to your mother." He quickly tried to push him away, but I pulled him back and whispered in his ear.

"Call, Luxe." I hoped and prayed that June didn't hear me. I could tell that Juju was scared, but I really wished he would try to be a big boy right now. Besides being scared for him and myself, I was also scared for Dynasty. That bitch Jazzy had hit her with a tire iron, and she was laid out cold at the park. I prayed someone had found her by now. I know Sebastian and Luxe are going crazy looking for us. The sun was coming up, and that meant we had been gone for quite some time.

"After everything I've done for you, I can't believe you would set me up. How could you, Leilani?"

"Let's get some shit straight, June. I've dedicated my entire teenage and adult life to being with you. I was under the façade that it was all about me, you, and our son. That was, until your fake ass death when I found out that your ass was married with children. So, please don't sit across from me trying to play the victim. I've been a victim since the moment you paid Dot for me. From the bottom of your heart, you know that I wouldn't cross you. You're the only man that I loved up until I met Luxe. All of this shit that you're doing is because you know that nigga has my heart, and I know for a fact I have his."

I don't know what came over me, but I knew I had said the wrong thing. June stood up from where he was sitting and walked closer to me. At the same time, I could slightly hear Juju talking in the other room. I knew he had called Luxe, and I was mad at his ass, but I knew he was the only way would make it out of this shit alive.

"That nigga got your heart, huh?"

"Hell yeah! I love, Luxe." I got loud on purpose in the hopes that Luxe would hear me. June drew back and punched me square in the nose, and I knew that he had broken my shit. He jumped up and went into the other room. He came back out dragging Juju and tossed him on the floor beside me.

"What's good? Big bad ass Luxe. You thought you was just gonna live happily ever after with my blocks and my bitch."

"Nigga, you pussy! Let them go, and we can do whatever. If you want to shoot it out, we can nigga. If war is what you want, nigga me and my brothers trained to go! On my life, nigga, and on the St. Pierre blood that runs through my veins, if you have hurt them in any way, I'm killing everything near and dear to you, and that's my word."

Tears streamed down my face hearing Luxe speak. I knew then this was so much more than him just killing June and using me as bait. If I were bait, he wouldn't give two fucks about him having us.

"Your mother wasn't lying; this hoe got you gone. I'm not mad at you. It's the pussy and that good ass head she got on her shoulders. You should be thanking me, nigga. I taught her everything she knows.

"You taught her, but I made her a pro at it." Was these niggas really sitting here arguing about who taught me how to fuck and suck a dick? I had to cover Juju's ears, because he had heard enough filth for a day."

"You got that. I'm gone have to test that shit out when I hang up. You love this bitch and my son. Well, come see me then, nigga."

"You motherfucking right! I love them both, and I'mma go to war with your ass behind mine. I'm coming Leilani baby. Believe that shit." June quickly hung up and yanked me up by my hair. He dragged me into the other room kicking and screaming. He slammed me down on the bed and started ripping my clothes off of me.

"Don't do this, June. Our son is in the other room."

"Shut the fuck up!" He started to roughly bite all on my breasts. At the same time, I could feel him trying to enter me.

4

"Really, nigga? You about to fuck her like I'm not even in the house, so all this shit I've been doing was to help your ass bring this trick back to you." June stopped in his tracks at the sound of Maya's voice. We both looked at her, and she had a gun pointed at us.

"Put that fucking gun down! June jumped up and headed towards Maya. At the same time, Juju came running full speed ahead through the door to get to me. It was like in slow motion that I saw Maya turn the gun on him and fire. The force of the bullet was so powerful that it sent him flying into the wall. This bitch had shot my baby.

Chapter One

June

"Nooo!" Leilani released a gut-wrenching scream from the pits of her soul as she frantically stood from the bed, ass out and all, not giving a damn about anything else going on around her. Her petite frame, appeared to be so fragile, so broken in spirit as she cried out in pain. Her long, curly hair was now matted to her head, and her beautiful face was ashen and stained with fear. Any other time I would see her caramel skin naked I would automatically brick, but this moment was bitter... not sweet.

Scrambling to her feet, she moved as fast as she could, but it became harder to function with each step. The closer she got to Juju, the weaker her legs became, and she fell forward onto her knees. Unable to bring herself to stand, she anxiously crawled towards Juju, and I could see her jittery hands as they shook uncontrollably. Juju, her only child's, limp body was lying face down on the floor surrounded by a puddle of blood. Only a few seconds had passed, but it felt like hours before she finally made it to him. Afraid, she hysterically lifted him into her arms and held him close to her chest, while she prayed loudly and rocked him back and forth.

Satisfied, Maya then turned her gun on me, "After all I've done for you, June; this is how you fucking repay me? By betraying me? You were gonna just rape this skank bitch like I wasn't sitting in the next room. I'm your wife, not her. Me, muthafucka. Meeee!" Maya paced the floor in front of me with tears of rage pouring from her eyes. "I feel so fucking stupid. Look at all the shit I went through for you. I've killed people and all kinds of shit for you, and you choose her!" She stopped and waved her gun in my face as if an epiphany hit her. "This wasn't about revenge on Luxe for shooting you; this was because he was fucking your side bitch. You fucking used me and I'm gonna kill all you muthafuckas! Fuck you, fuck that whore, and fuck your bastard ass son. I hope I killed that lil son of a bitch."

From my peripheral, I heartbrokenly watched the entire scene unfold, while I stood frozen, unable to move an inch. For some odd reason, I couldn't wrap my head around the fact that Maya had shot my son. Deep down inside of my heart of stone, I know I hadn't been the best dad to Juju, and I also know that I'd taken him and his mother through a lot over the course of these past few months, but I never intended for him to get hurt. To be truthful, I only spanked him out of spite because I didn't wanna hear him keep asking about that hoe ass nigga, Luxe. Juju came out my nut sacks. I made him with love, and I'm his only got damn daddy; he had to know that.

"So you just gone stand there and ignore me muthafucka!" Maya screamed, gun pointed directly in my face.

With each horrific word that Maya spoke, the initial shock that had taken over me was slowly diminishing and being replaced with anger. I couldn't take it anymore; the venomous words that viciously spewed from between her ratchet lips caused me to snap. Throwing my right hand over my shoulder, I slapped Maya so hard that her neck violently jerked backward, and she flew into the wall. At that point, I didn't give a damn about Maya or the gun that she held in her hand; she was gonna have to shoot me.

Quickly rushing her before she came back to her senses, I slapped the pistol from her hand, and it slid across the hardwood floor. Lifting her small frame into the air, I roughly slammed her back into the wall once more. With my large hands now wrapped around Maya's neck, I breathed bouts of dragon-like fire through my nostrils. All I could see was red, and I was draining all the life out of that miserable bitch.

"You hurt my son. My mutha fucking son, bitch!" I kept repeating, as I squeezed her long neck tighter and tighter.

To no avail, she raggedly gasped for air and clawed at my hands to try and break free. Shit like this was one of the reasons why I couldn't be with her trifling ass. This bitch was nuts, and even more so if she thought she was gonna get away with what she just did to Juju. While I choked her out, I scolded myself because I knew I should've left her ass when I had the chance. If I had, none of this shit would've ever happened. But nah, I had to be greedy, and being that she knew about everything I had going on, it was damn near impossible to leave her.

I met Maya fifteen years ago, shortly after I started messing with Leilani. Since Leilani was younger and her mother had given me complete control over her, it was easy for me to keep them apart. When it came to Maya, she knew I was a street nigga and she loved money, so it wasn't often she asked my whereabouts or even asked me to come home. However, Leilani was a different ballgame. The majority of my free time was spent with her, and putting her in charge of the club helped out a lot, because she was super busy.

Back to Maya, I met her one year after the feds did a big raid and bled the streets dry of product. That major drought had all the dope boys shook and most of the other connects scared to move, but Maya… that bitch was bold. Her nigga left her with a shit load of work and little money, so she was trying to eat by any means. She still took risks that many others were scared to take. At the time, I was looking for a new connect, so my homeboy, Rich, turned me onto to her. From what I gathered from him, her dude was doing football numbers in the feds, so she was running things to stay afloat.

Immediately, the wheels in my head started turning, and I devised a plan for a hostile takeover. Initially, I was just gonna have my partner set up a meeting to rob and kill her ass, but that all changed once I laid eyes on her.

Standing at five foot six, cocoa butter skin, long hair that hang to the middle of her back, and full, pouty lips, that bitch was bad, and I had to have her. My partners tried warning me about her, saying that she and her man were both off their rocker, but I didn't give a damn. All I saw was a come-up.

Shit was getting tight, and my money had almost drawn up, so all I was scoring was one kilo and with that, I was still barely making enough money to keep up the lifestyle I had grown accustomed to. Shit was all bad. True indeed, at first, Maya tried to play hard to get, but the more I kept coming back, the more I was spending. Once she saw the way I was handling my business in the streets, she started flirting with me. To not appear desperate, I shot her down a few times, but that did nothing but make her want me even more. However, when I did finally decided I had played the game long enough, I was all in. All it took was one night of putting this dick down and whispering sweet nothings in her ear, and I was able to finesse her out of everything she had. Over the course of six months, I got her to leave her nigga high and dry. She stopped sending mail, she stopped visiting, no more packages were being delivered, and he was no longer getting money on his books. His well had completely run dry.

After I had got him out the way, it was time to get a hold of her connect, and that's where Ava St. Pierre came in. She was one of the most ruthless bitches I had ever met in my life, but she didn't intimidate me one bit. At our very first meeting, she blew out the brains of a nigga that had crossed her right in front of me, but I didn't flinch nor bat an eye. Shit, I had done a lot worse to niggas that owed me a lot less.

"Help… me… momma." I heard Juju whisper faintly, and from the crook of my eye, I saw a sly grin tug at the corner of Maya's mouth.

With my eyes fully trained on the smirk on Maya's face, I completely zoned out and didn't hear Leilani as she crept to the side of me.

Pow! Pow! Pow!

Leilani shot Maya in the face. Shocked, I quickly released her body and watched it as it dropped to the floor. Wiping blood and brain matter from my face with my sleeve, I turned to face Leilani, and just as it was with Maya, she now had the gun trained on me.

"Put the weapon down, Leilani. We need to get Juju to the hospital." I begged.

With tears streaming down her face, her chest heaved up and down as she spoke, "How could you do all of this to me? I loved you and would have done anything for you. Anything! You took everything from me and let your wife put me out with nothing. Me and my son had no fucking where to go." she screamed.

I looked at her like she had two fucking heads. I know she knows damn well I wouldn't sit around and watch Maya do that shit to her.

"Fuck you, Leilani! When have I ever left you and Juju stuck out? When? The majority of the time I put y'all priorities above my wife and my other children." I gritted.

"I can't fucking tell! Where the fuck was you?"

"As if you didn't notice, I was shot the fuck up. I was in a coma for weeks and didn't know a damn thing. I didn't even know if I was going to live! I was nowhere around when Maya did that shit!"

Seeing the pain behind her eyes almost crushed a nigga. I know I had beat her ass, but it was only because she was sleeping with the enemy, and I didn't know whether she was in on it or not. And as far as Maya goes, I didn't find out what she did to Leilani until I made it back in town. Had I known, it wouldn't have played out like that. One thing for certain, and two things for sure, I never lied to Maya one time about my feelings for Leilani; she did know about Leilani from the very beginning, but she chose to play her role. I told her about everything from the jump, and we hadn't been in love with each other in years. Hell, I don't even think we were ever in love. We were only still together for the sake of our kids. Everything that bitch did to Leilani was out of spite, because she knew who my heart belonged to. You best believe I beat the fuck out of her when I found out, too.

I glanced over at Juju and then back to Leilani, "I never meant for anything to happen to him. Despite what you may think, I love that lil nigga and you too."

"Is this what the fuck you call love?" she gritted.

"You hurt me, too, Lei; come on now. You sleeping with the enemy."

Pow!

She shot me in the arm, "Bitch! I didn't know about any enemies nor your little family, and while you were on your little vacation, I hurt for you, I cried for you, and now look at what y'all did to my baby."

Grabbing hold of my aching arm, I stumbled backward and fought to keep my balance.

"Just calm down." I reached my good arm out to her, and she stepped back.

"Ain't not fucking keep calm nigga. My baby is hurting."

"That's my son, too, Lei!" I screamed. "I'm hurting, too."

Upon hearing my words, her face transformed to one of stone, and she quickly wiped away her tears, "Not as much as it's gonna hurt me to do this."

Pow! Pow! Pow!

The impact from the shots to my chest sent me flying into the air. My head hit the end of the nightstand, and I immediately blacked out.

Chapter Two

Leilani

As soon as June's body hit the floor, and I knew he was unconscious, I jumped up and grabbed my baby. I was naked as the day I was born when I ran out of the house they were holding us in. I didn't give a fuck. Right then, my only concern was getting my baby the help that he needed. Tears soaked my face when I realized he had stopped moving or making any noises.

"Please don't leave me, Juju! Mama is getting you some help right now! Please, somebody, help me! Help me! My son has been shot!" I was screaming and running down the street like a crazy person. As a matter of fact, I was a crazy person. I was a mother who was trying to save her son's life, and God had to definitely be on my side, because a police car that was riding down the street saw us and quickly stopped to help. Seeing that there was no time to wait for an ambulance, they placed us in the back of the squad car, turned on the lights, and pressed the pedal to the metal.

The entire way over to the hospital, I rocked Juju back and forth while talking to him and hoping I would get some type of response. When I saw his arm flinch, I knew right then there was a God, and he heard my prayers. Followed by the slight movements, I could hear him lowly moaning in agony, and it was still faint as hell. As if we were one, I could feel my baby slipping away, and that shit made me cry harder as I held onto him. My head leaned up against his forehead, and my tears were soaking his little face. If I could, I would've transferred every bit of his pain into my body; I swear I would. All my life, I believed in a higher power, but I had never prayed to God so hard in all my years. I needed the man upstairs more than ever.

Juju's fire engine red face had started to get pale, his lips, were turning blue, and his skin felt clammy. My baby… my poor baby, needed help now, but I couldn't panic, because I didn't want him to get scared. Before I knew it, the police had got us over to the hospital in record time. Seeing the hospital staff outside waiting for us made me somewhat happy because they could immediately get to work on my baby.

"He's not breathing!" I screamed out, completely hysterical. Snatching him from my arms, they lifted his fragile body onto the gurney, and then took off with me rushing behind them as they worked hard at keeping him alive. My whole world was spinning, and everything around me was happening so fast, that I could barely keep up. It wasn't until I heard him blueline when I came back out of the fog I was in.

"Help him please; save my baby." I screamed.

"Step back, ma'am!" A doctor yelled, and I watched them put the defibrillator on my baby's chest and shock him, not once, but three times before his heart started to beat again.

16

"We got him back!" The same doctor shouted as they rushed him to the back and disappeared through the double doors.

"Oh my! Look at you. Come on over here and let me look at you. While I make sure that you're okay, I need you to fill out the necessary paperwork for your son to receive the proper treatment." One of the nurses grabbed me by the arm and placed a sheet over me. So much was going on that I didn't realize that I was still naked. I didn't care, though, because all I could do was cry my eyes out. As soon as I got inside of the room, the same police officer who picked Juju and me up, and one of his colleagues, stepped inside. Immediately, my antennas went up, and inside I begin to panic, but I held my composure.

"Ma'am, we need to ask you some questions. How did your son get shot?"

Before speaking, I thought long and hard about his question. I knew that I couldn't tell these police officers who did this to my son. After all, I had killed Maya and June. Not to mention, Jazzy was somewhere on the run. Now that I think about it, that bitch was nowhere in sight when I ran out of the house. Just thinking about her ass made me think about Dynasty and wonder if she was okay. I knew that by me taking too long to answer, I was starting to look suspicious. Then it popped in my mind that my nigga ran the city. The damn police force was on his fucking payroll.

"Can I please call my son's father, Luxe St. Pierre?" I asked and then watched as the police officer who was asking the question leaned over and whispered in his partner's ear. After that, the partner left out immediately.

"Why didn't you say that shit when I first scooped you and little man up? Don't talk to anyone about this. I have everything under control. Here, call that nigga Luxe and tell him where you at. Also, let him know Officer Dexter is here taking care of you."

He didn't have to tell me twice; I hurriedly snatched the phone from his hand and dialed Luxe's number. The moment he picked up the phone, tears streamed down my face.

"Please, Luxe baby! Come to the hospital. Juju and I need you." I cried.

"I'm on the way, Ma. Stop crying. Are you guys okay?"

"She shot him! June's wife shot my baby!"

I started to cry again uncontrollably. Seeing that I was having a nervous breakdown, Officer Dexter grabbed the phone from my hand and walked out of the room. Although I was on the brink of going crazy, just hearing my baby Luxe's voice made me feel better, because I knew he was coming for me. Now all I needed was for my lil baby to be okay.

From there, they escorted me to my own room, and I was glad that the nurses were periodically checking on me and keeping me updated with Juju's progress. Otherwise, I probably would've had a stroke. As I laid on the bed trying to stay calm and wait for Luxe to get here, I could hear somebody snapping in a couple of rooms down, so I immediately got out of the bed and hauled ass out of the room. I would know that voice anywhere. It was Dynasty, and she was raising hell.

"I'm not playing; let me the fuck out of here! I need to get out of here and make sure my friend is okay!" she screamed.

"Dynasty!" I yelled, as I ran into the room where she was being held. They had her strapped to the railings of the bed. Her head was wrapped up, and blood was seeping through the bandage.

"Oh my God! I'm so glad you're okay. Where is Juju?" She cried.

"He's upstairs in surgery. Maya shot him in the chest. Friend, I'm so scared." I said, and we both cried for I don't know how long. Since she couldn't hug me back, I bent down to where she was and held onto her for support.

Looking at the bed, I tried to see if I could unhook her, but they had her ass locked in with a key to make sure she couldn't get free.

"I'm sorry I can't get you out of this shit. I will get them on top of it as soon as I leave out."

"It's gonna be okay, sis. They can't hold me down." She reassured me, as more tears leaked from her eyes.

"I know they can't, and I do believe it will be alright." I replied as I touched her hand. "But what happened to you? How did you get here?"

"Sad to say, I had been lying in that damn park unconscious all day. Some kids walking home from school found me and called the police. Lil evil fuckers saved my life. It's no telling what would have happened to me if I had laid out there any longer."

"I'm glad we don't even have to worry about that now. You're all good."

"Yea, but I need these muthafuckas to unstrap me." She yelled, loud enough for the nurses to hear.

Hearing Luxe in the hallway going crazy looking for me, I stood from my seat. I spoke over my shoulder as I headed for the door, "Give me two minutes, I'm gonna get Luxe on it right now. You won't be strapped down for long."

"Good, because I got some shit I need to handle, and being in this muthafucka ain't gone get it done." She replied, and I chuckled, because I already knew she was about to tear up some shit.

Chapter Three

Luxe

Hearing my baby cry like that had a nigga on ten. That nigga June had played me too close, and I was ready to murder the motherfucking city. That, on top of finding out that nigga lived had me baffled as a muthafucka. I distinctly remember emptying the full clip into his body and watching him take his last breath. How he lived is beyond me. Before then, I had never missed a target, and never not killed a muthafucka that I set out to kill. He had to have help.

I already had all my goonies on deck flooding the city trying to find my fucking family. Yes, Leilani and Juju were my motherfucking family. We had built a life together in such a short period, and the thought of losing either of them infuriated the fuck out of me.

"Where she at Bro? Did she say Dynasty was with her?" Sebastian was also on ten, because we still hadn't heard anything from Dynasty, and my nigga was having the hardest time. He was starting to feel stupid as fuck for allowing Jazzy back into his life. Just when he and Dynasty made shit official, he let Jazzy's hoe ass come in and shake shit up. I just pray we find her safe and sound, because Sebastian is gonna make the streets bleed until he finds out where she's at.

"She didn't say Bro. Let's get up to the hospital. That bitch Maya shot Juju."

We were already in the car busting blocks looking for them, so we made a U-turn and headed straight to the hospital. The entire ride over, I prayed to God my lil nigga Juju would make it out of this shit. Leilani loved that little boy more than anything in this world, and it would kill me if he didn't survive.

*****

"Where the fuck is my girl? Leilani baby, where you at?" I started to go crazy when the nurse took me to the room she was supposed to be in, and she wasn't there. All types of shit was going through my head.

"I'm right here, Bae." She ran to me, and I hugged her tightly. Her words were inaudible as she cried on my shoulder. I pulled her back and lifted her chin so that I could look into her eyes while I spoke.

"Shhh! Don't cry. I'm gonna handle everything. Juju is a fighter, and he's gonna be okay. Listen to me, Leilani. There are people all around looking and listening to us, so I need you to pull it together. Let's go back in the room that they had you in. I need for you to tell me everything that happened from beginning to end. That's the only way I'm gonna be able to find these motherfuckers."

"First, I needed you to get them to unstrap Dynasty, now. They've been taking too long, and you know she bout ready to fuck shit up in here."

22

"Where she at?" I asked as I released her.

"She's two rooms down." She pointed.

"Alright, I'm on that now." I walked away and headed to the nurses' station to handle the situation with Dynasty.

Upon seeing me re-enter the room, Leilani immediately began talking, "I killed them." She said barely above a whisper.

"Can you remember where that nigga was holding you and Juju?"

She nodded her head yes, and I hugged her tight and kissed her on the forehead for comfort.

Sebastian burst in the room, "Hey, Sis! I'm so glad that you're okay. Nephew is gone be just fine. He's strong as hell. Please tell me you know where Dynasty at? I've been calling her phone, and she's not answering. I'm worried as fuck."

"Really, nigga? You worried about me all of a sudden. I think you got your bitches screwed up. Last time I checked you cared about that bitch Jazzy more than me, so nigga you can miss me with all that fake shit. As a matter fact, I suggest you go find that bitch before I do. I swear when I catch that hoe, I'm stomping mud holes in that bitch and putting a bullet in her fucking brain, and in case you didn't get the memo, fuck you too, nigga!" Dynasty suddenly appeared behind Sebastian, and I just knew it was about to be a war.

"You want me to fuck your ass up in here, Dynasty!" Sebastian looked like he wanted to murder her, as she slowly limped away in pain. Instead of Sebastian going after her, he picked up one of the recycling bins and launched it across the room as he left out the door. Security was scared as hell to move on Sebastian, and I wanted to go after him, but I couldn't.

"Ms. Brooks." A female nurse called out to Leilani.

She was accompanied by an older, male doctor who had on blue scrubs and a lab coat.

"Hello. I'm Dr. Shelby, and I've been overseeing your son's surgery. The bullet he sustained to his chest missed the heart by inches. However, it's lodged in his back by his spine. He's still in surgery, and we're working diligently to get it removed without doing any damage to the spine. The main issue is that we're having now is he's lost a lot of blood, and we've used all that we had in the bank for his blood type. We will need you or the father to give blood, and we need it asap; it's a matter of life or death for your son.

"He's A-positive like his father. I can't donate because I'm O negative." Leilani said, as she collapsed in my arms, and I was trying my best to hold her up. This shit was so fucked up. For the first time in my life, I felt completely helpless, but I swear if I had to, I would drag motherfuckers in here off the street to get my little nigga the blood he needed.

"Shhhh! Stop crying, Leilani. We'll find some blood that matches. Calm down before you make yourself sick." I lifted her up and placed her in a chair.

"Excuse me I need to see a doctor. I've been shot." I looked up when I heard the familiar voice. To my surprise, it was non-other than this fuck nigga June holding his arm. Without thinking twice, I took off running towards that nigga and started beating his ass.

"Noooo, Luxe! We need his blood for Juju." It was like hearing Leilani say that made me stop beating the shit out of him. That, and the fact that the hospital police were now placing me in handcuffs.

"Sir, you cannot go around attacking patients?" Security said, and I laughed in his face.

"This ain't over you bitch ass nigga!" I said, as they restrained me.

"I'm back, nigga. I'm here for my blocks and my family." Hearing that, I went crazy. While they held me tightly, I watched this motherfucker head over to Leilani and yank her arm, and she quickly drew back and slapped the shit out of him.

Chapter Four

Dynasty

Seeing Sebastian's handsome face almost calmed the beast in me… but then, I remembered how he played me to the left for that fake ass bitch, Jazzy. That hoe hit me with a mother fucking tire iron in my head. Nah, she's not getting away with no shit like that. Bitch tried to take me out but failed miserably. The worst thing she could have done was left me alive, because now I'm on that ass, and it ain't nothing anyone can do or say to make me change my mind. I don't give no fucks that she's Jr's momma; I'll just have to live with taking his momma out. As much as I would hate to never be a part of Sebastian's life, if he tries to interfere, I'm gonna fuck him up, too. There was only so much I can take. People have been playing me too close all of my life, and I'm tired of letting shit slide.

As I stood in my hospital room staring out the window, my mind was consumed with nothing but murderous thoughts. I just couldn't believe that June had allowed Maya to shoot Juju; that's my godson, my baby, and I love him with everything in me as if he were my own. June got to go, too! I just hope Leilani will be ready to murk his ass when the time comes, because shit has gotten way out of hand. Damn, my kill list had gone from zero to one hundred real quick.

The door crept open, so I slowly turned to see who was coming inside. When I saw Sebastian's pitiful face, I turned my back to him; now was definitely not the time.

"Please talk to me, Dynasty. I know I fucked up. I'm sorry. It's just that so many things are happening right now. I need you." He pleaded.

"Umph," I grunted, but that was about all he was getting from me.

"I never meant to hurt you, and I'd never do it again if you give me a chance to make everything up to you."

"It's too late for all that. You should've had my back the way I had yours." I screamed, becoming upset all over again.

His head fell to his chest, and he stepped closer to me, but I held my hand up to halt him. His touch, always one that I craved, was something that I wasn't ready for. Especially, not at this moment.

"I'm gone ask you to leave. I'm not feeling none of this shit right now."

"But Dynasty…"

I interrupted him from speaking any further, "No 'but Dynasty', nothing! I don't wanna hear shit! Just go, Sebastian."

In a rage, he flipped over the food tray and stepped into my personal space against my wishes. His tall stature towered over me, and his smooth, chocolate skin almost made my mouth water, but then I remembered that I wasn't fucking with him. He wore a crazed look in his eyes, which turned me on, but I kept it G. Now that I think about it, when he's mad, he looks just like Morris Chestnut on *The Best Man,* except he had more muscle. *Damn, this nigga sexy as fuck when he's angry.*

Dressed in his usual Ralph Polo attire, he looked preppy but hood at the same damn time. However, I stared at him defiantly, because no matter how sore my body was, if he laid one finger on me, we were gone tear this room up. I mean that with everything in me.

"You can try to push me away all you want to, but I'm not going nowhere so you might as well cut the fucking attitude. I apologized for my dumb ass mistake, and now I'm gonna do whatever is in my power to make it right and your stubborn ass is gonna let me."

Caught completely off guard by his words, I threw my head back in a fit of laughter. Who the fuck did he think he was?

"Boy bye, get out and go find your baby momma, because if I find her first, that bitch is as good as dead, and I mean that."

"That's the second time you've said that to me. What the fuck is going on Dynasty? I know you don't like her, but is it enough to make you want to kill her?"

"Hell yea it is! Why the fuck do you think I'm here? Do you think I did this shit to myself? Look at me!" I pointed to the bandage around my head and then to my face."

"So you saying Jazzy had something to do with this?"

Getting into his face, I looked him square in the eyes, "She has everything to do with this, and it's all your damn fault. You the reason she got to get so close to the family and learn all of our damn business. Did you know that the bitch was meeting with Maya, June's wife, every Saturday night when she thought we were sleeping?"

He rubbed his hand down his face like he did anytime he was bothered, "How do you know?"

"I busted her ass sneaking in a few times, but I wasn't sure exactly where she had been because she would be dressed up and smell of liquor. I figured maybe she was gone to an after hours spot or something. It wasn't until I followed her from the club, that I actually found out what she was doing?" I laughed in his face once again, "Has she even contacted you or came to see about her child since I had been missing?"

He shook his head no and slowly sat on the edge of the hospital bed.

"Didn't you find that shit strange or were you too blinded by that fake ass puppy love that you hanging onto?" He stared blankly at me, unable to speak. "That's what the fuck I thought. Now get the fuck out my room."

With his shoulders slumped in defeat, he stood from the bed and walked toward the door. Sadly, he looked over his shoulder into my stern face before he grabbed the doorknob and spoke, "I'm gone make this right, even if I have to kill Jazzy myself. I love you, Dynasty." And with that, he left.

I hated to see him go, but I couldn't bear to look at him any longer, and I meant every word I said when I told him that it was his fault. I love him, I really do, but I can't help but feel like he was the main reason they were able to get so close. Sebastian's a sweet man, and he loves hard, and that's one of the things that separates him from his brothers, but that very trait can also get us hurt. He has to do better and have his eyes wide open at all times. He should trust no one; not even me if he ever thinks that I'm doing anything shady behind his back. I damn sure wouldn't trust him.

Quickly, I removed the IV from my arm and threw on my shoes. Since I didn't have any fresh clothes, my hospital gown would have to do; I needed to get as far away from the hospital as I could to clear my head. Right now, I'm a ticking time bomb, and that's not good for anyone around me. I hate to leave Leilani at the hospital, but it's only gonna be for a short amount of time. I hope she understands.

I'll be got damn. I got to be seeing shit. I whispered, in disbelief as I made my way towards Juju's room.

My eye twitched in anger, and unconsciously, I reached for my hip where my gun would usually be carried, but it wasn't there. I forgot I left that shit in my car at the park; that will never happen again.

31

June pulled Leilani's arm, "I'll give him some blood if you suck this dick for old time's sake."

"Fuck you!" she screamed, while snatching her arm away. "You are a real live hoe ass nigga, and I wish I killed your bitch ass back at the house." She gritted.

"But you missed, baby girl; next time, aim for the head. The odds of killing me are better." He chuckled.

"Don't worry, I will do just that next time."

Stepping back into my hospital room, I looked all over for something to attack his fat ass, and the only thing I saw was a metal bed pan, so that's exactly what I went for. Weighing it in my hand, it wasn't too heavy, but it wasn't too light, and the metal looked durable enough to do some damage, so I was pleased. Seeing that it was just right, I headed out the door and straight for June. He had me fucked up.

While Leilani and June stood there going back and forth, they were so engrossed in their conversation that they didn't see me coming, and that was just what I needed. Since this son of a bitch thought it was cute to let those hoes hit me with a tire iron, I thought it was cute for me to bang his ass up, too. No sooner than he opened his mouth to say something else, I hit that motherfucker in the back of the head so hard that he fell into Leilani. Being that his slick talk had already pissed her off, she was all in. While I tore his ass up from behind, she was raining blows over his head. He tried to fight back, but he wasn't a match for two angry ass women, and we weren't letting up.

From behind, security tackled me to the floor, and we tussled. I wasn't gonna let him just put no damn cuffs on me. I had every right to bang June's ass up. Security was a big, burly motherfucker, and my little ass was no match, but do you think I cared... nope. He was getting the best of me, but shit wasn't easy.

"Get the fuck off her." Sebastian snatched the security guard up and threw him into the nurses' table.

Afterward, he went in on June with Leilani since they were still over there fighting. Being that the security guard had gotten mad at how Sebastian handled him, he tried to rush him, but I stuck my foot out to trip him, and Sebastian threw a mean uppercut putting him on his ass.

"The police are on their way up to take all y'all to jail." A nurse threatened.

"Well, I might as well whoop your ass, too." I shot back, as I savagely approached her table but Sebastian yanked me up.

Sebastian was right on time, too, and I wanted to thank him, but fuck that, he owed me that much. Luxe stepped off the elevator with the police to find the whole area in an uproar. Before the police could get to Leilani, he scooped her up in his arms, and then the officer grabbed Sebastian.

"I'm going to have to ask y'all to leave. We can't be having this nonsense going on in here." The police officer said while waving a nurse over to check on June, who was on the floor snoring like a muthafucka.

Since there was no way I could get to June to stomp his ass out some more, I hawked up a glob of spit and spat it right on his face. Fuck that bitch ass nigga! That's for my baby Juju.

"Sebastian, grab your girl and get her out of here before they take her ass to jail." Luxe winked at me, and I could tell he was pleased with the moves I made.

Sebastian grabbed my arm to make sure I was okay, but I snatched away, "Just take me to go get my car. I got it from there."

Chapter Five

Sebastian

Dynasty quietly sat in the passenger's seat of my Range Rover not saying a word, and that was just fine with me. I had already got on my knees like Keith Sweat begging for forgiveness, but I'm not gone keep making myself look like a sucker. She was gonna either get with the program on her own, or I was gonna make her whether she wanted to or not.

"Where we going? My car's at Rochester Park." She stated, with an attitude.

Ignoring her, I continued heading toward my house like she hadn't said anything.

Since I wasn't paying her no mind, she roughly tapped my shoulder, "I know you hear me, Sebastian. Just take me to my car; I don't wanna go to your house."

"Shut the fuck up and ride Dynasty. You might as well get whatever it is in your head that you think you about to do, out. I'm not letting you out my got damn sight."

"I don't need you to fucking watch over me. I'm not a kid." She crossed her arms over her chest.

"Now correct me if I'm wrong, because I think I'm missing something, but could you please enlighten me as to where I asked you to meet me that night after the club?"

Feigning ignorance, she shrugged her shoulders and turned her head to look out the window, but I grabbed ahold of her face and made her look at me.

"I'm waiting."

She rolled her eyes and mumbled so low that I could barely hear, "You told me to meet you at your crib."

"And what did you do?"

"Don't try to turn this shit on me!" she screamed, furiously.

"Just answer the question, baby. What did you do?"

She blew out a hard breath, "I followed Jazzy, but I had to. The timing was just right, and if I hadn't, there's no telling what would've happened to us."

"You right, and I thank you for being on your toes, but you can't blame all of the shit that happened to you on me. I called you several times, sent messages, and had other people call you for me, but you cut your damn phone off. You didn't want me to know what the fuck you was doing, so I suggest you stop pointing the finger and take some responsibility for your actions. You're partially to blame for this shit as well." I stated, matter of factly.

From the corner of my eye, I watched her face as it changed from just being pissed to one of the devil, and then out of nowhere, she hit me in my face so hard that my head jerked sideways and hit the window. With my free arm, I tried to hold her back, but there wasn't much I could do since I was driving, and she took full advantage by continuously throwing punches my way.

"So you wanna blame me, nigga! Nah, fuck that." She hissed, as she threw another jab to my jaw.

Fed up, I pushed her face as hard as I could to get her ass off me, but she kept right on coming. Frustrated, I quickly swerved into the right lane and pulled the car over to the shoulder of the highway. After slamming the car in park, I released my seatbelt, and just as I was diving into the passenger's side to fuck her up, that bitch kicked me in the mouth. Dazed, I fell back into my seat and touched my blood-stained lips. I was hurt, but it wasn't until I saw the blood on my fingers that I became enraged. It was time to get out and kick her ass, so I grabbed the door handle, let myself out, and then ran around to the passenger's side. That bitch was gonna make me kill her!

She's a bold bitch, too; any sane woman would have tried to lock herself inside, but nooo, she didn't even reach for the locks. It was as if she was waiting for me to run up on her ass. Snatching the door open, I furiously grabbed her shirt to pull her out the car, and she reared back and socked me in the eye. I ain't gone lie, that shit hurt like a muthafucka, but I wasn't releasing the grip I had on her ass for nothing. After getting her all the way out of the door, I grabbed her neck and lifted her off her feet. Not wanting to let me get the best of her, she grabbed hold of my neck, and we were choking the hell out of each other. It wasn't until I slammed her back against the metal railing that she let go. By now, I was sick of her and this tough-guy shit. She was responsible for some shit, too. All she had to do was call me when she saw them together, but nah, she wanted to handle things her way.

"Bitch! If you hit me one more muthafucking time, I'm gone throw your ass over this rail, and you gone swim with the muthafucking fishes." I gritted, blood dripping from my mouth onto her gown.

She grinned, "Do it, do it, Sebastian. I dare you."

Looking down into her face, I had mixed emotions. On the one hand, I wanted to toss her ass, but on the other, I knew she was mad at me for a reason.

"You really think I won't throw yo ass, don't ya?"

"All it is to it is to do it. I'm waiting. I ain't never flown before, so this gone be my lucky day."

Hearing her reply, all I could do was smile; Dynasty was crazy as a muthafucka, and I loved that shit. It was funny, because I was the chill one out of my brothers, but I got the craziest bitch. While she sneered at me, I placed my lips to hers and kissed the shit out of her.

"Chill out, girl. We 'bout to go home." I said, as I lifted her from the railing and placed her on her feet. "Don't be like that Dy; I love you."

She rolled her eyes and hopped in the car, but didn't say anything else for the remainder of the ride. As long as she wasn't putting up any more fight about my decision to take her back to my place, I was cool. She should know me better than that; it's too much shit going on in these streets, and I didn't feel comfortable with her not being around me. Bad enough I already felt awful for not being there to protect her.

****

"What the fuck!" I whispered, to myself as I opened the door. All my things were scattered everywhere; the house was a complete disaster. On high alert, I turned to Dynasty, "Stay right here while I go check things out to make sure nobody else is in there."

"Where is Jr.?" she asked, frantically.

"Fuck man; I left him here with the Nanny," I said, and then turned to leave, but she grabbed hold of my arm.

"If one goes; we both go. You know better than that."

Seeing that I wasn't gonna change her mind, I entered further into the house with her right on my heels, and a cloud of smoke hit us smack dab in the face. The further into the house we traveled, the smokier it became, and we had to cover our eyes to keep them from stinging. After a few moments of inhaling the smoke, a burning sensation built in my chest, and I couldn't contain my coughing. The kitchen was just a little ways up, so I was damn near running to go check and see what was going on.

"Griselda must've been cooking. That's chicken burning on the stove." Dynasty informed me while opening a window and then the rear door.

As long as it wasn't a fire, my nerves had calmed a little but not much because I still didn't see Jr. While she handled things in there, I stepped into the hallway and ran straight for the stairs, heart pounding and nerves going crazy. All I wanted to do was find Jr and Griselda okay. My heart beat out of my chest as I turned the knob to Jr's room to find him sitting in the corner, tears coming down his cheeks. After picking him up, I placed kisses all over his face; I was happy to see him in one piece.

"Where's GeGe?" I asked for Griselda by the name he had given her.

He laid his head on my shoulder and pointed towards the closet, "She's in there. Mommy told me not to let her out, or she was gonna whoop me."

I quickly sat him down on the floor and ran to the closet, and as soon as the light hit Griselda's face, her head snapped up, and she started mumbling something. However, her mouth was covered with duct tape so I couldn't understand what she was trying to say. They had tied her up and really had did a number on the sweet lady. *I'm gone kill that bitch Jazzy.* I thought to myself. After untying Griselda's hands and wrists, I helped her out of the closet and to the bed so she could sit.

With tears streaming from her eyes, she grabbed hold of my face, "You such a sweet man, but have bad choice women. Jazzy is evil; she kills you if chance."

"Was there anyone else with her?"

"Yes." He nodded her head. "Two men."

"Sebastian! You may want to get in here." Dynasty yelled, and I stood from my kneeling position.

"Okay!" I replied. "You two stay right here. I'll be right back after I make sure everything is cool for y'all to come out."

I briskly walked into my room not knowing what to expect. Jazzy had already done some fucked up shit to Griselda, so I could only imagine what she's done in there.

"Look at this shit!" She screamed at me while standing in the door of our closet. "That dirty bitch took my clothes! Damn near all of them, too."

I heard her fussing about her clothes. However, that was the last thing on my mind; I needed to get to my safe. Pushing her out of the way, I rushed inside the closet and threw all of my clothes off the hangers. I didn't need nothing in the way of me getting to my stash. I hurriedly typed in the code and snatched the door open, and what I saw next knocked the wind out of me. Jazzy had wiped me out. Everything in there was gone except for a folded piece of paper, so I snatched it up and read it out loud.

Checkmate Bitch! Have fun raising your son. I'm out!
Sincerely yours,
Jazzy

"I'm gonna kill that bitch," I screamed and then turned to Dynasty, who stood off to the side with a smirk on her face trying to keep from laughing.

"You better not say shit!" I stormed past her.

"Oh, I'm not. You've already got that ass spanked hard enough." She cracked.

"Fuck you, Dynasty!" I replied as I sat on the bed.

Her head snapped in my direction, and she was looking at me like I was doing something wrong.

"Okay, okay, it's understood the love of your life wiped you clean, and someone's been in the house, but now they're gone, so you can get your ass up and go get my car. Thank ya!" She snatched up her under clothes and headed to the restroom to shower.

Chapter Six

Diamond

"Ms. Johnson! Wake up." I quickly jumped up feeling someone shaking me. I looked all around the room for Shawn.

"Did you see him? He tried to smother me!" I cried out of breath. The nurse was looking at me like I was crazy. The dream I had was so real. Shawn had got into my hospital room some type of way and placed a pillow over my face. I was scared as fuck, because that meant he was still out in the world. I just prayed he left me alone, because I'm not giving his ass another dime. I was shaking so damn hard I needed to grab onto the bedrail.

"I'm sorry no one has been in here since your husband left. I'm here to take your vitals. It's also time for you to feed the baby. Are you okay? Would you like me to give you something to eat? The baby can be fed in the nursery if you're too tired."

"No. I'm fine. Thank you." I held back tears as she took my vitals. At the same time, I looked off into the distance at my newborn son asleep in his bed. Out of everything that has occurred in my life, he was the best thing that had ever happened to me. I can't believe that I wanted to get an abortion. From the moment I gave birth, I'd been asking God to forgive me for even thinking about some shit like that.

"Here you go. He's so handsome. Hit the call button if you need me." She handed me a fresh bottle and my son at the same time. He was the splitting image of Judah. It was crazy how he had his entire face. Not to mention his feet and toes. I swear Judah marked my baby with all his bullshit.

"As long as I live JJ, you will always come first in my life. I promise to be the best momma in the world to you. I love you more than anything in this world. As long as I have life inside of me, I will protect you from any and all harm. You're my young Prince, and I'm gone raise you to be a great King. When I look at you, I see greatness."

I stared into my son's beautiful, gray eyes and spoke to him as if he understood. I just wanted to put greatness into the universe for the both of us. I had a funny feeling it would most likely only be him and me anyway. I was just bracing myself for the blow that I knew is coming. It's not just me anymore. I now have someone to look after. Judah St. Pierre, Jr. has given me a boost of strength that no one would see coming.

*****

I sat in the lobby of the hospital waiting for Judah to arrive so he could take us home. I was more than ready to get away from the hospital and sleep in my own damn bed. I was also ready to get to Leilani. I had missed a lot of shit being in the hospital giving birth. She needed my support more than ever, and I felt like I wasn't being a good friend by not being there with her. No matter what was going in her life, Leilani would drop whatever she was doing to come support me or just be a shoulder for me to cry on so, without a doubt, I had to be there for Boss Lady. She saved my life on several occasions.

I was glad that Juju was doing much better. When I talked to Leilani over the phone she told me that after Dynasty had knocked the shit out of June, they were finally able to get the blood they needed from him. At the time, Juju was in a medically-induced coma and had a good chance of surviving, so hearing that calmed my nerves a bit. I still can't believe that nigga allowed that bitch Maya to hurt him. I'm just glad Leilani offed her ass. I wish she would have killed June's ass, too, because now his ass is out in the streets loose again.

After donating the blood to Juju, that motherfucker cut out. Now his ass in hiding. That's exactly what he had better do, too because the St. Pierre Boyz were on that ass. Shit was about to get real for him and that bitch Jazzy too. Dynasty's ass was on all types of good bullshit looking for her. I've always known her to be a thoroughbred, but right now she's in straight beast mode. She doesn't take shit from nobody so for Jazzy to hit her with a tire iron, I knew she couldn't handle that shit. Dynasty is out for blood, and I pray she catch that scandalous hoe and rock her ass to sleep.

*****

"Do you have everything you need before I drop you off?" Judah asked, as he snatched the car seat off my lap.

"No, I have everything." I replied, still sitting in the wheelchair as the nurse wheeled me out front to the car. Judah placed our son in the backseat and made sure he was secure and I was moving slower than usual, because my pussy was so damn sore. I had gotten stitches, and that shit had me itching and burning. I couldn't wait to get home and take a Sitz bath. Once I was in the passenger's seat and strapped in, Judah quickly drove off. I felt so uncomfortable sitting next to him, and I felt it coming before he did it. Judah reached over and slapped me so hard that my head bounced off the window.

"You gave that fuck nigga my money. I know ya bitch ass didn't think I forgot about that shit, ole deceitful, hoe ass."

I held my face in shock at the fact that Judah would hit me while our newborn son sat in the backseat. Feeling the guilt of my betrayal weighing heavily on my shoulders, I blew his actions off and apologized.

"I'm sorry. I was scared and didn't want to risk Shawn showing you those pictures and exposing me. It was stupid of me, but I did what I thought was gonna keep us together."

"Nah, you didn't do a motherfucking thing for us; your snake ass did it for you, but you love me, though."

"I do love you, Judah!" I cried, as I reached out to touch his hand.

"Get your motherfucking hands off me before I slap your ass again." He spoke through gritted teeth.

From the remainder of the ride I kept my head turned looking out of the window until we pulled up to the house. Before the car even came to a complete stop, he jumped out and grabbed the car seat and the bags, and I would be lying if I said I wasn't afraid to go inside the house.

Judah was looking like he had murder in his eyes, but I finally built up enough courage to go inside. Rushing pass him, I quickly walked over to the couch so that I could sit down because I was hurting and he wasn't trying to offer me any assistance.

Moments later, Judah came downstairs with his Louis Vuitton luggage.

"Where are you going?"

"I'm not going anywhere; this is your shit. Did you actually think that I would allow you to stay in my house? Bitch, you can't be trusted. The only reason your ass is still living is because of my son. This here ain't working out between us. I'm done with your lying, conniving ass, and you can stop with all those crocodile tears because they don't mean shit to me."

Hearing that, I quickly wiped my face, because at that moment I realized I was making a fool out of myself by showing him how much I cared for his ass.

"You're absolutely right, Judah. It's not working out between us. For some reason, you think I need you. Nigga, I don't need you. I want you, and that's the motherfucking difference. In case you forgot, I had my own everything when

I met your ass. I've been taking care of myself for a long time, Judah, so you putting me out don't mean shit to me. With your immature ass. You're a momma's boy. All that tough shit is a façade. I don't want no nigga who is fake as fuck. You can hit me but look over the shit your dead ass momma was pulling. That bitch fucked you up in the head."

"I'll beat your ass in here, Diamond. Watch your mouth!"

He swiftly, walked towards me like he was about to hit me. I flinched a little, but I held my stance.

"Do it. I guarantee you we will be rocking in this motherfucker. That slap you just delivered in the car is the last time you will ever put your fucking hands on me. I don't know why I've allowed you to beat me this long, but this shit is over, finito, and finished. From the bottom of my heart, Judah, you don't ever have to worry about my son or me."

"Don't threaten me with my son. I'll take him from you, and you'll never see him again. Don't fuck with me, Diamond. When I get back, I want your ass gone. I've set up the townhouse in the city for you and JJ. You already know whatever you need I got him. I don't have to be with your ass for me to be a father to my son."

He walked over to the car seat and kissed our son on the forehead before walking out of the house. How dare his bitch ass; did this nigga really think I would leave his home peacefully? That nigga about to pay for every time he put his hands on me and for all the times he straight disrespected me. I grabbed my son, and placed him in his car seat before walking back in the house to grab my bags. After putting them in the trunk, I went back inside and then to the garage. I grabbed a can of gasoline and walked all through the house pouring that shit everywhere.

"You want to play with me, motherfucker! Like I'm the enemy! I'm about to make you hate me. I lit a match and threw it inside his closet because that's the first thing I wanted to burn. The house was quickly becoming engulfed in flames. As I casually walked out of the house towards my car, I hopped on Snapchat. I looked at myself and ran my fingers through my hair as I made duck lips making sure to have his house in the background on fire. Before I uploaded it, I wrote the caption:

He played with my heart, So I burned his house down!!!

I hopped in my car and headed straight to the townhouse he wanted me to stay in. I wasn't hiding, running, or ducking shit. Fuck Judah and fuck Shawn if they wanted a war I was about to give it to the both of they ass. Ain't no more fucking over Diamond. That shit is dead as fuck.

******

The sound of someone banging on my door made me jump out of my sleep. I grabbed Lucille, my pearl handled .22, off the dresser before heading towards the door. I knew it was most likely Judah, and I was ready for his ass. I peeped over at Judah, Jr., and he was still sleeping soundly. I then slowly made my way towards the door and glanced through the peephole.

"Bitch open this damn door. I can see you looking through the peephole."

I quickly opened the door seeing that it was Dynasty.

"I thought you were, Judah," I said as I sat my gun on the coffee table and sat down on the couch.

"Bitchhhhhhh! You done had that baby and done lost your mind. Toting guns and burning down houses and shit. That's what the fuck I'm talking about!" Dynasty was hype as fuck. She was all for this type of shit. I just shook my head at her as she picked up my gun and started playing with it. I love my friend, but this bitch was off.

"I didn't want to do it. That nigga left me no choice. Judah slapped the shit out of me when were in the car bringing home JJ. Then, when we made it in the house, he comes walking downstairs with luggage. I thought he was leaving until he said I was the one leaving. That shit turned me into a demon, and before I knew it, I was pouring gasoline all over the house. I'm officially done with him thinking he can handle me any kind of way. I'm not some random ass bitch. I'm the mother of his child, and he will start giving me the respect that I deserve. Until then, it's war, and I'm ready for whatever." I replied while watching Dynasty dab at her eyes.

"Bitch, what the hell is wrong with you?" I asked as I looked at this fool and she appeared to be crying.

"I'm so fucking proud of you, Left Eye! I knew underneath all that soft shit was a beast." I couldn't do shit but laugh as she pulled me in for a hug.

"Judah has brought out the worse in me with his bullshit, and I can't take it no more. I love him, but I for damn sure don't need him. Fuck him."

"We're on the same page. I love Sebastian, but I'm not fucking with him, period. He had let that bitch Jazzy come into our lives and ruin everything. I'm good on his ass."

"Their mother fucked them up," I said, as I headed into the kitchen to grab my phone off the charger.

I looked at my notifications, and Judah had sent me numerous texts talking about how he was gonna kill me. He had called me well over a hundred times, but I didn't care. As I scrolled down my notifications, I saw an inbox from my mother, Liz. That's the only way she could get in contact with me, because I refused to give her crack head ass my number. I grabbed the counter and held on to it reading her message. My grandmother had passed. The funeral was the upcoming weekend, and I needed to get home to Chicago for the services.

"Are you cool, Boo?" Dynasty asked.

"Not really. My grandmother is dead." I let tears fall down my face because knowing she was dead made me realize I didn't have anybody. My Grandma Brenda raised me on the

Southside of Chicago. Despite battling Cancer off and on, she managed to take care of me and my two older brothers Kilo and Bam. Bam got killed when he was eighteen, and Kilo was sentenced to ten years in Federal Prison for Drug Trafficking. It's like, after that happened, her health deteriorated. She could no longer take care of me, so the first chance I got, I picked a place on the map to start a new life and that just happened to be Dallas. As my luck would have it, I ran into Shawn's ass and the rest is history.

Just the thought of going back to Chicago hurt me to the core. All it did was remind me of all the pain and heartache that I left behind. I missed Bam every day of my life. He never really got to live, because he was too busy trying to run up behind Kilo. Niggas from out west wanted Kilo dead, and since they couldn't get to him, they got at Bam to send a message. We got the message loud and clear, because losing Bam dismantled our entire existence. I didn't even realize I was shedding tears until I was on the floor and Dynasty was consoling me.

"Shhhh!" Everything is gonna be okay. You go to Chicago, and I'll keep Lil Judah. He will be just fine. It's too soon for him to be traveling on a damn airplane. I love you, friend."

"I love you, too. I don't know where I would be without you and Leilani." I said, as I hugged her tightly. It was true; my life had been better since I met them. They were the true definition of friends. I just wanted to enjoy the birth of my son, and now I had to leave him and go to Chicago to watch my grandmother be lowered into the ground. This shit was about to be a bitter ass pill to swallow.

Chapter Seven

Judah

As soon as I saw Diamond I was gon' murder her ass, and it wouldn't be long before I caught up with her. The only thing that was keeping me from kicking in her door was the fact that my son was in there. That, and the fact that my brothers were on my ass about trying to get at her. I hate to admit it, but I was on some 'fuck them' type of shit, too. Don't get me wrong, I love my brothers with everything inside of me, but they do shit without asking my opinion first. Last time I checked, Ava was all of our mom. What gave Luxe the right to kill her? Of course, she deserved it, but we should have all decided that she had to go. Not just his ass.

My brothers didn't understand the impact that her death has had on me. Out of all us, we had the strongest bond. I don't think it was ever any real love on her part, but I loved my OG. Now that I know what she was capable of, I know that she didn't love me. All of that shit she used on me was manipulation tactics on her part. She knew she couldn't easily manipulate Luxe or Sebastian, so I was the weakest link. Now, it has me questioning my entire existence.

It's like our whole life had been one big ass lie. A façade that she put on. Not to mention the fact that Luxe held in the fact that nothing was wrong with her crazy ass. I feel like such a fool going to that nursing home and begging her to talk to me. It hurt a nigga heart to know that she knew nothing was wrong and allowed me to pour my heart out to her. That was some cold-hearted shit for her to do. Then for her to turn around and try to bring harm to the girls. That shit was out of line.

I just keep seeing her black, cold eyes as she went above and beyond to expose Diamond. It didn't matter that she was pregnant with her grandchild, or the fact that her son loved this girl more than anything in this world. Ava was all out for herself and didn't care who she had to hurt to eliminate people. The more I sat and thought about it, the more I realized that six feet under is where she needed to be. I just hate that it happened the way it did, and we didn't find out the evil that lurked inside of the woman who gave us life until it was too late.

****

I sat inside of the meeting with my brothers, there, but really not there. My mind was on my son, my house, and most importantly, Diamond. I was so fucking mad that I wanted to fly down to the Chi and put her ass in a plot next to her grandma.

"You cool over there, Lil Bro?" Luxe asked.

"Do it look like I'm cool, nigga? In case you missed the memo, my motherfucking house was burned to the ground, and I lost everything." I snapped.

"Pipe the fuck down, Judah! I understand you in your feelings, but get over that shit. Your ass is a millionaire; you can replace all that shit; that shit irrelevant. We got bigger stuff to worry about. Like, where the fuck is this nigga June at. I'm not resting until I find that fuck nigga. What he touched was mine, and he got to come see me about that. I need your head in this shit, Judah; we are now the head niggas in charge of the St. Pierre Cartel. Tighten up, Ju."

Just hearing Luxe talk like that put a lot of shit into perspective. I definitely needed to handle this street shit and fuck Diamond up later.

"I got a lot of shit going on right now, Bro, but you know I'm ten toes down and ready for whatever." I replied.

"That's what the fuck I'm talking about, Lil Bro. This nigga got to die for all this shit. Him and that bitch Jazzy got to go. Not only was the bitch in cahoots with June the whole time, but that bitch also hurt Dynasty, and the scandalous ass bitch abandoned our son. I don't give a fuck about what she stole from me. She can have all that shit, but that hoe got to die for ever thinking she could cross me and get away with the shit." Sebastian jumped in, heatedly.

Sebastian was pissed; I could tell by the way that his veins was sticking out the side of his neck, but at the same time, it was funny as hell. We had told him that bitch Jazzy was up to no good and not to fuck with her. Now he sitting here wanting to kill that bitch. I got ready to speak, but Luxe's phone rang, and I couldn't really read his face, so I waited for him to hang up.

"You okay, Bro?" I asked.

"That was Leilani. Juju woke up and was asking for me. We'll handle this later. I need to get down there to see my lil man. In the meantime, your ass needs to hop a flight to the Chi and be with Diamond. She needs you right now, Bro."

"I agree, Lil Bro. Dynasty got JJ. Just go on ahead and do a pop-up. Make shit right before it's too late. Your ass gone be walking around here like me begging like Keith Sweat." Sebastian added.

I was hearing what them niggas was saying, but I wasn't trying to listen to that shit. If I saw Diamond, I might beat her ass. I was pissed about her burning my shit down, and I needed to calm down before I laid eyes on her. I didn't even say shit to my brothers; I just got up and left. The only thing that would probably make me feel better would be my son. All of this fucking anger I have pent up inside of me had been blocking me from loving on him. Just because I was mad at his mother didn't mean I had to take it out on him.

*****

"Don't come over here on no bullshit, Judah. I'm in an ass kicking mood, and you deserve a well-whooped ass. I could really bust you across your head for your behavior."

"I'm not on no bullshit. Calm down, Killa. I just came to see to see my Jr."

Dynasty shook her head and stepped to the side to let me inside of her house. Looking at her I couldn't help but to think about how my brother had his damn hands full with this crazy ass girl. She had me fucked up, though, if she thought I was gonna let her pull them stunts with me. I'm not Sebastian. I will knock her ass out. Dynasty is not a damn woman; that's all man right there. Shaking her threat off, I walked into the living room and picked my son up out of his car seat.

"What up, Lil Nigga?" I spoke and placed a kiss on his forehead before I sat on the couch with him.

Just holding my twin calmed me down some. Looking at him made me think about Diamond. He looked like me but had her skin tone and a nice grade of hair. My Jr. was gone be catching all the pussy. Bitches love a nigga with some good hair. I'll make sure to never allow Diamond to cut it.

"Have you talked to Diamond?"

"Nope, and I'm not trying to either," I said but kept my eyes trained on my son.

"You really need to stop with all of your bullshit, Judah. My friend don't deserve what the fuck you do to her. What the fuck is wrong with you St. Pierre brothers? You niggas have three of the baddest bitches rocking for y'all. One thing I know about me and my bitches, we go hard for our niggas. What you motherfuckers don't understand is that we don't need y'all. We want y'all. That's the difference. I know I'm a handful, and niggas out here can't handle me. However, your brother can. That's what I love about him, but I can't allow him to treat me like I'm nothing. I deserve better than that shit he pulled with Jazzy.

His behavior has me questioning his loyalty. Up until he chose that bitch Jazzy over me, I trusted him with my whole heart, but now I'm not convinced he deserves it. I'm saying all that to say this… you better stop being so fucking abusive to my friend. Diamond has had it rough all of her life. The way you treat her only adds to her lack of self-confidence. Your treatment of her has driven her over the edge. She's burning down your house and carrying a gun in one hand and her baby in another around the house. That shit ain't cool, Judah. Diamond is a soft-hearted and gentle person. You've turned my friend into a demon. Let me ask you something. Do you love her?"

"Yeah, I love her."

I didn't even hesitate when I answered, because I know that I love her. I think that's what had me acting so crazy with her ass.

"If you love her, then you need to be in Chicago supporting her. If you don't feel like you should be there, then you need to leave my girl alone for real Bro. The next time you put your hands on her, I swear we beating your ass, Judah, and you know I ain't scared of no nigga. Seriously, though. Go out there and support her. Losing her grandmother really hurt her. I got JJ. Don't even call her just show up. That will make her day."

I sat in silence listening to Dynasty, and made up my in my mind that she was right. I couldn't believe I let her talk me into it, but I was heading out there.

"I'm gonna go, but I'm still mad about her burning my house up."

"Oh, get over it, and buy a new one."

It was so fucked up that everybody thought that Diamond burning my house down was nothing. All my fucking, clothes, jewelry, and furniture was gone. That shit was expensive. I kissed my son one last time and got ready to head to the Chi.

Chapter Eight

Jazzy

Babyyy! After seeing Leilani shoot Maya in the face, not one, but three times, these long legs of mine had a mind of their own, and before I knew it, I was hightailing it down the street in my Escalade. When I heard that first shot, I had got up to go see what was going on, and when I rounded the corner, I saw her getting all Gangsta Boo. That in itself was enough for me to want to save my own life… fuck them. I don't give a damn if people judge me or not. You can call me scary or whatever else you wanna call me, but there was no way I was sticking around to see if I was gonna be next. That heifer had gone crazy after Maya shot her baby, and I can't say that I blamed her. That was grounds for her to put holes in everybody in the house, including me, considering I helped get them there. Shit had gotten too hot in Texas for me to stick around, so my best bet was to get away for a while.

Before going to Sebastian's house, I called to see if he was there, and when Griselda told me he wasn't, I called up a couple of niggas I met around the way, and we went over there to hit that easy lick. Those fools didn't know what it felt like to get some real money, so when I offered them five stacks, they were more than ready to do whatever. For me, robbing Sebastian was nothing; I didn't even break a sweat. However, it pained me to have to leave Jr. behind, but it was better off that way. I didn't want to have to travel from state to state and be on the run with my baby. It just wasn't safe for him. If anything popped off, I wanted to make sure he was out of harm's way. I'd die if I had to experience the same thing that Leilani was going through.

It took me a week to figure out where I would go, but as soon as I found my next destination, I was out of there. Pulling my thin blazer tighter around my body, I exited the plane at LaGuardia Airport and made my way to baggage claim to grab my things. After pulling the last bag off the carousel, I reached in my pocket, retrieved my phone, and then scrolled the log for Don Don's phone number so I could let him know that I was in his city.

Speaking of Don Don, he was Maya's brother and my bae. We'd been going at it for over a year now. Although we didn't get to see each other often, whenever we hooked up, you couldn't tell that we'd missed any time away from one another. I must admit, he was a little rough around the edges, but he was still a good dude. I really liked him, and I think he liked me just as much. However, sometimes his ass was mean and had a funny way of showing it. Right now, I'm hoping he'd be just as happy to see me as I was about seeing him; I *am* popping up without calling.

"Yo!" his answered, on about the fifth ring. "What up Ma, what brings you to ring me up at this time of morning,"

Looking down at my watch, I saw that it was one AM; I forgot we were on an hour time difference.

I licked my lips and brushed a loose strand of hair behind my ear, before I nervously replied, "I'm in your neck of the woods, and I was hoping we could spend some time together."

"Word," he replied, casually.

"Word," I nodded my head as if he could see me. "I'm at LaGuardia; could you pick me up or do I need to catch a cab."

"Nah, Ma, you good; I'm only about ten minutes away. Meet me at the front," and with that, he hung up.

Smiling, I grabbed the handles on my bags and hurriedly pushed my way through the crowded airport so that I could be there when he pulled up, which didn't happen. From where I was, it took me all of twenty minutes to make it to the exit, and when I finally did, he wasn't there, so I started to panic. Stepping outside, my head traveled from side to side in search of his vehicle. Right when I was about to pull my phone out to call him, an Ocellus teal 2016 Ashton Martin pulled alongside the curb in front of me. Since I didn't know what kind of vehicle he was in, I stepped away from the curb just in case it was someone else.

A few moments later, the back window rolled down, and Don Don motioned with his finger for me to come over to him.

Placing my hand on my hip, I eyed him to see if he would at least offer me some assistance. After all of thirty seconds had passed, and he hadn't gotten out of the car, I decided to speak on it.

"Can a girl get some type of help with her bags," I pointed at the four suitcases that were on the ground by my feet.

He chuckled like I had said something funny, while shaking his head, "The only help you can get is the help you been having. You better chunk that shit in the back and let's go before your ass have to catch a cab; I gotta shake a move."

Glaring madly at Don Don and his Congo looking ass driver, who had done a poor job of hiding his amusement, I stomped to the trunk, threw my luggage inside, and then slammed it.

"Don't get fucked up," Don Don warned, accent thick as hell, as I slid in the passenger seat.

Leaning over to give him a peck on the cheek, I replied, "It's good to see you, too."

Before my glossed lips got to meet his skin, he covered the side of his face with his hand, and I gently kissed the back of it on accident, "Stop that shit! I don't know what your ass be in Texas doing."

"Are you serious right now?" I asked, partially hurt by his reaction.

He placed a blunt to his lips, lit it, and pulled hard on it before blowing the smoke in my face, "Dead ass!"

"You don't be worried about that any other time," I pouted, while batting my lashes and twirling my finger in my hair.

He looked down at his diamond-encrusted Rolex, then to me, and then took another pull.

"You buggin, Ma; a nigga don't be sober, either."

I heard him talking that hot shit; however, as I took in all of him, I suddenly became distracted. This man had the most unique rustic red skin that I had ever seen with a perfect set of white teeth, and he was as tall as a pro ball player. With chiseled arms and tight abs, he could clearly be an underwear model for the biggest brands. His dark eyes, so penetrating, so domineering, captured me each time he looked my way, and I had to fight my urges to steer clear of temptation.

His hair was in a low cut and on his face was a thick beard; he was sexy as hell, and not to mention, he was paid. Looking down at his apparel, they weren't shabby either, and I love a well-dressed man. Covering all his sexiness was a green Lacoste polo shirt, a pair of black Lacoste jeans, with none other than wheat Timberlands on his feet. He wore no jewelry beside his watch, and he didn't need any either; you could tell he was loaded with cash without it.

Leaning back in my seat, I decided not to argue with him; I needed him on my side right now in case somebody came looking for me. A sister didn't need any more trouble than what she already had. While gazing out the window, he rubbed the back of my neck, and then I heard his zipper slide down. Knowing exactly what he wanted, I smirked slyly, and my mouth began to water upon seeing his hard tool standing up at attention.

"Come on, Ma; you know what a nigga like." He licked his lips and then began massaging the back of my neck.

Slurping loudly, I made sure to suck him like I missed him, all sloppy, wet, and nasty. He never could last long when I sucked him off, so only after a few minutes in, he was releasing his kids down my throat to the abortion clinic. Feeling satisfied, he patted my head like a puppy and zipped his pants.

"Now that that's out the way, I got something I need to ask you," he studied my face, as he slowly poured himself a shot of Remy Black and then took a sip. Patting his chest where it burned, he frowned his face and placed his cup in the holder. "Now back to what I was saying. I need to ask you a few questions."

"Go ahead," I replied, as I slowly walked my fingers down the length of his thigh.

My panties were soaked, wanting to feel him inside me; I loved pleasing him. I got off every time.

Moving my hand away from his thigh, he glared at me, "Where's Maya? Me and Killa Kaam been calling all week, and we have yet to hear from her."

I shifted my eyes towards the window, while I nervously tried to think of the best lie I could, "I don't know, baby. I haven't spoken to her in a while myself. We had a falling out over something minor, and you know we both are too stubborn to call."

"Yea, okay," he took another toke of his blunt. "Yo word is bond until I find out something different," he blew his smoke in my face.

Since I wanted to kick it with Don Don for the day, he took me with him to Killa Kaam's lounge, and I wasn't too excited about that. Although Killa Kaam was handsome as fuck, putting me in the mind of Camron from Dip Set, he was even ruder than Don Don, and he had no respect for women. Anytime we would be around each other, there would be a huge elephant in the room; at least for me, it was.

Looking down at the phone in Don Don's hand, I discreetly watched him dial Maya's number a few times, while I rubbed his shoulders.

After the fifth time, the voicemail picked up, he became frustrated and slammed his phone on Killa Kaam's desk, "This shit's mad annoying son."

Killa Kaam looked from me to Don Don, and then back to me again, before speaking, "Shit just isn't adding up to me."

"Me, neither," Don Don agreed. "And I'm really starting to get pissed off."

Killa Kaam ice grilled me before calling his goon over, "Yo, get this bitch the fuck out chea so we can talk. I'on trust her ass."

I placed my hands on my hips, "You don't have to be so rude, K. It would be great if you would give me a fair chance. I'm good people."

He laughed, "Anytime a bitch got to try to convince you she's good people, then she's the total fucking opposite. Good people give off good vibes, and I don't get that from you."

Before I got to reply, Don Don waved his hand, dismissing me, and I twisted on out of the room without so much as a peep. One way or another, I was gone be in on the conversation; I needed to stay ten toes ahead. Slightly pulling the door closed, I left a big enough crack for me to see and hear.

Killa Kaam leaned forward, placed his elbows on the desk, and interlocked his fingers while staring at the door, "Yo, that bitch is mad grimy son."

Don Don nodded his head, "I think so, too. She must think a nigga crazy or some," he laughed. "Any other time I asked the bitch to come up north, she declined, but now she's here out of the blue. I'm gonna keep an eye on the snake."

"Meanwhile, I want you to gather up some of our best shooters and make a trip to Texas while I stay back and finish handling business. You know that shipment from the new connect is coming in, so I need to make sure everything runs smoothly."

"Cool, but what do you want me to do about Jazzy," Don Don asked.

"Take that bitch with you. Fuck she staying here for?"

"Word!"

Don Don nodded his head and inside I began to panic. If I got caught on TX soil I was good as dead, and if I ran from them, I was also good as dead. Fuck man, I'm damned if I do and damned if I don't.

Chapter Nine

June

I inhaled another toke of my blunt, and as the purple haze clouded my intimate thoughts, my mind kept wandering to the day I was shot. If Ava hadn't had her men there to save me, I would've been a goner, because Luxe didn't stop shooting until the clip was empty. To this day, I could still see the evil in that niggas eyes as he pumped hot steel into a nigga's flesh. Although I tried to appear to be tough, that shit fucked with me, and the nightmares often woke me from my sleep fully drenched in sweat. The only way I was going to get over that shit was if I put that nigga in the dirt like he tried to do me.

Fucked up part about everything was that it was the son who shot me, and the momma who saved my life. How ironic is that? The last thing I remember was Luxe standing over me with his gun pointed directly at my head. He told me he'd see me in hell and then pulled the trigger but it clicked, there were no more bullets in the gun. With blood-stained teeth, I grinned mockingly at him and then he hit me over the head, knocking me out. Two weeks later, I finally woke up from my coma, and I was in an unfamiliar place with Ava St. Pierre sitting on the side of my bed.

When I asked her what had happened and where I was she glared as she told me to not worry about all that. From what she had told me, I was dead to the world. Her doctor friend had shot me up with a medicine called Tetrodoxin that put me in a coma-like state, and a funeral was given for me and everything. Hearing that shit blew me the fuck away as I laid in bed staring off into space while taking it all in. Suddenly, a feeling of paranoia came over me, and I tried to move, but she had me strapped to the bed. My heart was racing and I just knew I was gonna be dead soon; I couldn't trust her ass.

If you let her tell it, she spared my life because she needed me to take out her sons. At first, my interest was only in killing Luxe, but after she had offered me the streets for their lives, I became interested. Plus, she spared no details when she told me how Luxe was with my bitch. She stated that her plans were to wipe any trace of the St. Pierre clan from the territory so she could bring over the Baptiste Mafia with no extra problems.

While I daydreamed, my daughter stood in my face trying to get my attention. Her lips were moving, but I couldn't hear her speak a word as I stared at her cinnamon skin and freckled face. Those were my lips that kept running a mile per minute, but her mother's eyes staring into my face. I must admit; she was a beautiful mixture of Maya and me.

"Did you hear me, Daddy." She shook my arm causing me to snap out of my daze.

"What did you say Ja'Mya?" I asked, after clearing my throat.

She placed her hand on her hip, "Daddy, I asked where my momma is. Why hasn't she been home?"

I didn't want to keep lying to her, but I had no choice. What would I say? Your mother shot the brother you had no clue about, and his momma killed your mother; fuck out of here.

I grabbed her arm, pulled her to me, and planted a kiss on her forehead, "She'll be home soon." I lied. "She went on a little vacation because she needed some mommy time to herself."

As if the wheels were turning in her little mind, she searched my face for the truth. Her eyes, so penetrating, so inquisitive, were making me feel uneasy as a dagger shot through my heart. I hated to lie to her; she was my heart. I gathered that this is what Leilani must've felt like.

The house phone rang for the hundredth time, so I reached around Ja'Mya and snatched it from the receiver. *Fuck man!* I mumbled, as I watched Maya's brother, Killa Kaam's, number flash across the screen. I hurriedly hit the end button, and lightly pushed Ja'Mya from in front of me; I needed to hit a line. The pressure was becoming too much to bear, and I didn't know how much longer I'd be able to stall everybody.

Killa Kaam and Don Don got shit on lock in Queens, New York, and I knew it would only be a matter of time before they came running down here to check on their sister.

75

"Daddy, daddy, somebody on the TV." Jah pointed to the monitor that was stationed to the right of me.

Quickly turning my head in the screen's direction, I spotted roughly about six nigga's running towards my house and my mind went into overload. Snatching my kids up in my arms, I ran up the steps to their room and placed them inside the closet.

"No matter what you hear, or how scared you get, don't come out this closet. Do you understand me?"

"Is this like that little game you and momma play with us?" Ja'Mya asked, with tears on the brink of falling.

Ja'Mya was a very smart girl, so I knew she would remember the emergency drills Maya and I used to have them doing in case something went horribly wrong.

"Yes, but this is real, and it's very important that you stay here. Daddy don't want you to get hurt." I replied, and then quickly placed a kiss to each of their foreheads before closing the door and locking them inside.

Running inside my room, I grabbed my twelve-gage pump from the side of my bed along with a few other pistols. Before heading out, my eyes zeroed in on the plate I had on the dresser filled with the purest cocaine on the streets. Sticking my whole face into the saucer, I inhaled as much as I could, and then stood upright. Feeling the effects of the drug come over me, I wiped my hand over my face and quickly ran to the bottom of the steps, gun pointed straight at the door.

Luxe had already caught me off guard once, and it wasn't happening again. My name is June, which is the hottest month of the year, and muthafuckas betta act like they know. I'mma set it off in this muthafucka! I'm feeling like Superman and Tony Montana all wrapped into one. These bitches can't fuck with me!

My heart raced as the drugs and adrenaline freshly pumped through my blood. Although I was a tad bit nervous, I wasn't afraid and would do anything to protect my life. Feeling the drainage dripping from my nose, I hurriedly wiped it away with my sleeve. My eyes, which were buck wild, scanned the room, and I became anxious. Right when I was about to step down to search the house, someone delivered a kick to the fragile door, and it came flying off the hinges.

Boom!

I let the shotgun roar, and the first guy who ran through my door got hit in the center of his chest and went flying into his people. Jumping over the rail, I stood to the side, sending shots at anybody coming my way.

This shit was some bullshit; this wasn't even the home we lived in, so I didn't know how those muthafuckas found me that fast. Feeling like Tony Montana, I talked shit while reloading my gun.

"You bitch ass niggas coming to my home with this shit? I'm killing every last one of you fuck boys."

Bullet after bullet was flying my way, and I was doing my best to dodge every one of them. However, while I was busy trying to get out of the way of one, there was another that grazed the side of my head and I grabbed at the spot while ducking for cover.

Hearing the fire cease, I stood from my crouching position, and aimed my twelve-gauge once more.

"I wouldn't fucking do that if I were you." Don Don warned, as he placed a gun to the back of my head. "Yo, drop the mutha fuckin gun, son, and drop it slow."

Gradually, I lowered the gun to the floor and placed my hands behind my head, while turning to face him with a mug on my face.

"What the fuck is up with this shit? My kids could've got hurt! You niggas don't know how to call before y'all come." I gritted.

Don Don stepped closer and put the barrel of the gun right between my eyes, "You don't get to ask no fucking questions, but you can answer one. Where the fuck is Maya, nigga?"

"Fuck you mean where Maya at?"

Don Don cocked his gun, "Nigga, you got three seconds to tell me something, or I'mma splatter your brains against the wall."

This nigga wasn't playing no games, so I had to think quick on my toes. After not giving it much thought, I said the first name that came to mind, "She with Jazzy, nigga. Why the fuck you ain't called…"

Before I got to finish my sentence, he hit me in the mouth with the gun so hard that it brought me to my knees, blood spaying from my mouth and nose.

"Bring Jazzy inside. This nigga just said Maya's with her." He smirked, and at that moment, I knew I was busted.

Moments later, a frightened Jazzy walked through the door with pleading eyes for me to tell the truth. Looking at her, I felt no pity; that bitch was a snake, too. However, I did think of something even better.

After spitting blood onto the floor and wiping my mouth, I looked Don Don square in the eyes, "I know I lied to you about Jazzy, but I'm only trying to save Maya's life. The St. Pierre Boyz took her, and I'm the only one who can get her back."

He sneered, "Nigga, that's my sister, and ain't no leaving without her. Fuck them niggas. Point me they way."

Chapter Ten

Leilani

I was so happy that my baby had finally woke up from the coma he was in. There were days, moments, hours, and minutes when I thought that I would never get to hear his voice or see his big, beautiful, brown eyes again, but now he's awake and out of the woods. I can't do nothing but thank God. It all felt like a dream, and even though this was my reality, I still couldn't believe this bitch had shot my baby. As a matter of fact, all the events surrounding my life were unbelievable. This shit had me questioning my sanity and people's real motives in my life. It was all so confusing, and I hadn't had time to really question things because Juju was my primary concern.

I know it sounds crazy, but I just didn't understand why June would go through this whole charade of being dead. For months after his "death," I could see him clear as day in his casket. That was him. I had so many questions, but I know that I will never get the answers I deserve. I needed closure, but I don't understand why. I guess it's because I loved this man up until his dying day; well at least what I thought was his dying day. Before then, if someone had told me June was a snake, I would have laughed at their ass. That man treated me like a Queen. There was nothing too expensive or extravagant for me. If I wanted it, he got it.

Just thinking of June being married made me cringe. My skin crawled at the thought of him loving someone else the way that he loved me. I swear I didn't want to think about him, but how could I not? Every time I look at my son, all I could see was the June I fell in love with, not the monster he'd turned into. I can't help but wonder if things still would've been this way if Luxe had not stepped in and changed our lives forever.

"Is Daddy coming to see me." Juju was trying to sit up to eat his Jell-O.

From the moment he woke up, he had been driving me crazy asking about where Luxe was at.

"Yeah, baby. He's coming. I called and let him know that you're woke and were asking for him. Just relax; he'll be here, Juju."

His eyes were wide with fear as he looked around the room, "He needs to hurry up before they come and shoot me again. Can you call him again, Ma, please? I'm scared."

He started to look like he was panicking, and I quickly jumped up to hug him so that he could calm down.

"Shhhh! They won't hurt you again. I promise."

"You're lying. You said Daddy died, but he came back and hurt us. I want Luxe!" He screamed and started thrashing around in the bed.

Luxe needed to hurry his ass up. It'd been hours since I called him. He should have been here by now.

****

2 hours later

"Hey, Daddy. I've been waiting for you to come forever." Juju was being so dramatic, but I could tell that he was happy to see Luxe, and it warmed my heart seeing them hug each other. Looking at the expression on Luxe's face, I could see that he was just as happy that Juju was awake and gonna be okay.

"Where have you been?" I gritted; he didn't know what Juju had been taking me through.

"I needed to handle some shit, and I just got done. Here, get him dressed; it's not safe here. Since they won't allow me to hire around the clock security, he's going home. Everything is all set up for him, and I even have around the clock care."

I heard everything Luxe was saying, but I couldn't help looking at him like he had lost his mind. Since Juju was my son, you would have thought he would run this shit by me first, and since he hadn't, I had gotten an attitude just that fast.

"Do you really think it's a good idea to move him, Luxe?"

"Look, this hospital is not secure enough for us to just be in this motherfucker, while he recuperating. Fuck that, he can go home and do it comfortably. I'll rest better with you and him being under around the clock surveillance. In case you

83

Mz. Lady P & Mesha Mesh

forgot, June and Jazzy are still out there plotting. I'm not taking any more chances, so please stop asking questions and get him ready, Leilani. I'll be downstairs making sure things are calm and secure." He shoved a bag in my hand with Juju's clothes in it and quickly walked out of the room.

I loved Luxe, but sometimes I hated how bossy and demanding he could be. This nigga had forgotten that I was Juju's mother, and that I had a fucking say so in his care. However, at the moment, I had too much on my mind, so I needed to remain calm. There was so much on my heart that I wanted to get off of it, but I didn't know how to approach Luxe. Forget it, I will just do it when the time was right. In the meantime, I will embrace the fact that my son is alive and well; despite June being on the loose. For some reason, I don't think he will come around fucking here with me anymore. Dynasty and I had beat the shit out his ass. Her crazy ass gave that nigga a concussion when she hit his ass with that bed pan.

About two hours later, we had arrived at the house, and just like Luxe said, he had made one of the guest bedrooms into a makeshift hospital room. Juju didn't care either way; as long as he was gone be able to be home with Luxe. I was exhausted; it had been weeks since I had slept in my bed, and I just wanted to relax.

"You good Bae?" Luxe asked as he walked out of the bathroom with a towel wrapped around his waist. Droplets of water cascaded down his chest. I couldn't help but get turned on just looking at him in all of his glory. Luxe was the epitome of a Greek God. I had so much on my plate and on my mind at the moment. Looking at his sexy ass made me forget my problems if only momentarily.

"Not really but I'm happy to be home. Just having Ju-Ju home and safe relieves some of the stress that I'm under."

"I have something that will help relieve some of that stress." Luxe dropped the towel and slow stroked his massive dick. He licked his lips seductively and walked over to the bed. He roughly grabbed me by my ankles and pulled me down to the edge of the bed. He spread my legs in the V shape and slipped his dick inside of me. It didn't take much for him to gain access . After all I was soaking wet off his touch alone. Luxe was hitting my soul with each thrust.

"I've missed you so much Babe." I moaned out in pleasure as he begin to speed up the pace. I would usually want to match stroke for stroke with Luxe but right now I just wanted him to have his way with me. I didn't have it in me to ride the shit out of his dick. At the moment I was like clay and he was molding me. I closed my eyes and bit my bottom lip as Luxe to me to heights of pleasure that was unimaginable. It was unbelievable how Luxe made love to my body. It was nothing that I had ever experienced before. Luxe and I have had sex plenty of times. He fucks a bitch so good he makes every time feel like the first time.

"I've missed you too. I love you Leilani." He said looking into my eyes. At the same time he came long and hard inside of me. For a couple of minutes he remained on top of me. I closed my eyes and rode the waves of ecstasy as I came all over his dick. Moments later he rolled over and I laid my head on his chest. Not long after he was snoring lightly. On the other hand I was wide awake and overthinking like crazy.

As I laid in bed next to Luxe, I couldn't help but wonder if he was genuine with his intentions with me. I never questioned it until I found out that he was behind what happened with June. In my heart, I want to believe that he fell in love with me out of the blue, but in my mind, I'm feeling like it was all a set-up to get back at June. As I closed my eyes, I prayed to God this man really loved me. It would kill my entire soul if I found out my son and I were nothing but a pawn in his game.

Chapter Eleven

Luxe

I had more shit on my plate than a little bit. It was like some shit was just brewing, and I could feel it in my soul. Things were about to get real funky, and bodies were about to start to dropping like flies, all courtesy of the St. Pierre Boyz. A nigga was not gonna be able to rest until I had murked that nigga June. There was no motherfucking way I could let that nigga get away twice. The first time I knew for sure that nigga June was dead when I hit his ass up and just thinking about him being alive made me angry all over again. Ava ass was still wreaking havoc from the grave.

Speaking of Ava. I had yet to inform my grandparents in Haiti about her death. I was trying to figure out the best way to let them know without looking guilty. Her parents held rank in Haiti, so I knew it would be a backlash behind it. That, added with the fact that my father's family, which are the St. Pierre's, have been at odds with my mother's family the Baptists since my father's death. They've always blamed my momma, and now that I know Ava, they had every right to be mad at her. Her ass killed my father.

I know that Judah is feeling some type of way about me killing Ava. I raised him up since a jit, so I know when he in his feelings. He might not understand now, but he'll thank me later. Ava couldn't continue breathing the same air as us. We would have never been able to enjoy the happiness that we deserved. Judah is a momma's boy, and it was a shame that Ava was never really a good mother. We were nothing but pieces in her Chess game against the St. Pierre Cartel. With her being dead, I was now officially Head of everything. There is no I in team, though, so this is not my Cartel alone.

This shit belongs to Sebastian, Judah, and me. We've all poured our blood, sweat, and tears into this shit over the years, so it's only right we run the shit equally. Of course, I'll remain the nigga who lays down the law. My brothers need structure when making decisions. They think off adrenaline. They'll have us all locked up doing hard time or dismantle the shit all together. They have an 'I don't give a fuck attitude', but that shit has to change. We're on a new level, so we have to move more precise and carefully.

Besides the street shit that was going on, I was happy as hell that Juju was home and out of harm's way. In such a short time, he had grown on me. That's my son, and no one can tell me differently.

Since I had picked Juju and Leilani up from the hospital, she had been acting off. As a matter of fact, since all of this shit has transpired, she's been standoffish. The shit wasn't sitting right with me, but I understand that she's just been through some traumatic shit. However, I have enough shit going on in the streets. The last thing I need is some shit between us. Out of everything that has happened, her and Juju give a nigga a purpose to keeping going.

"Leilani, come to my office, please," I spoke into the intercom system to alert Leilani that I needed her. The house was too damn massive to try and walk room to room to find her ass.

"Yeah." She said, with an attitude, as she walked inside of the office and sat down across from me. I had to hold my tongue, because her attitude was starting to piss me off to the point where I wanted to smack her ass.

"What's wrong?"

"Nothing." She said, as she kept her head down scrolling through her phone.

"Put your phone down when I'm talking to you. That's disrespectful as fuck, Leilani. You know I hate that shit." She blew out air in frustration and rolled her eyes.

"I need to go make dinner, Luxe. Is there a particular reason why you called me in here? I don't have time for this."

"Let's get some shit straight. First of all, watch who the fuck you talking to. I know they call you Boss Lady, but I'm Luxe St. Pierre. I'm gon' need you to put some motherfucking respect on my name. Second, of all, all that attitude and rolling of your eyes make you ugly as hell. Third of all, I need you to stop acting like a bitch and get whatever is bothering you off your fucking chest. If not, I advise you to stop walking around here with a chip on your shoulder before I give you a reason to be mad. I have enough shit going on right now, and I don't need this bullshit from you. Now, if you ain't got shit to say, you're dismissed."

I leaned back in my chair and flamed up the blunt that I had rolled in my blunt dish. I definitely needed to smoke after this shit. Leilani had me fucked up if she thought I was gonna keep allowing her ass to walk around with a fucking attitude. That shit was dead. She stood up to leave but quickly turned around and walked back over to my desk. I stood up cause she looked like she was about to hit me.

"Actually, there is something I need to get off of my chest. I just need to know why you shot June?" I bit the inside of my jaw and sat back in my chair. I toked the blunt real hard before I answered her.

"Now, I got a motherfucking attitude. I'm trying to see why you give a fuck. At the same time, don't worry about shit that don't concern you. I'm not asking why you was fucking that bitch ass nigga so don't ask me about why I tried to kill that motherfucker! You still love that fuck boi or something? Let me know now so I can see if you love him to death!"

I roared and placed my Glock on the desk with the barrel pointed at her ass. Say what you want about me, but I swear I would kill her ass if she answered wrong.

"Really, Luxe? I can't believe you're threatening me." Leilani looked like she wanted to cry, but I wasn't buying that shit. Her feelings were just hurt, because I checked her ass.

"I don't make threats. I make promises and follow through with them bitches. Now, I'm going to ask you one more time.

90

Do you still love that nigga?" I spoke through gritted teeth with the meanest mug on my face. I was done playing with her ass. She needed to answer the fucking question.

"No, Luxe. I don't still love June. As a matter of fact, I hate him. At the same time, I'm wondering about how we came to be. Was I a part of your game to kill June? Do you really love me and Juju, Luxe, or are you doing all of this to get back at June? Please don't be mad at me, but I have to know. One day my life was going great, and in the blink of an eye, it was changed forever. Everything I knew to be true became a lie after I had thought he died. Then, all of sudden, you appeared out of nowhere. Did you take care of us because you felt responsible for what I was going through?"

"Your ass is really funny to me right now. Are you seriously standing here questioning my intentions? If there is nothing else, that's true about me. I need you to know and understand the love I have for you and Juju is from the heart. For you to even question the shit, it lets me know you don't appreciate the nigga before you. Please don't get it fucked up, Leilani! I ain't never had to trick a bitch to fuck me. I'm a motherfucking St. Pierre. I've had bitches that paid to get this dick. Don't flatter yourself, Ma.

As far as your life going great before I stepped in, you and I both know that shit was built off of a lie. Fuck outta here. Trying to act like a nigga fucked your life up. If any motherfucking thing, I upgraded your stanking ass. I'll do us both a favor and fall all the way back from this shit we got going on. I refuse to lay up with a bitch that don't know my worth. As far as Juju, that's mines right there. It ain't shit I won't ever do for my little nigga. I still want to adopt him and give him my last name. As far as me and you go, I'm good. Relationships ain't for a nigga, anyway. You're free to go find that nigga June and rekindle your relationship. Here it is I'm trying to wife you, but you're more comfortable with being a mistress." I put the blunt out, grabbed my Glock, and placed it on the small of my back. I grabbed my kids and got ready to head out, but she grabbed my arm stopping me.

"Where are you going, Luxe? We're not done talking. I do love you." She cried.

"Get you motherfucking hand off me!" I jerked my arm away from her ass so hard I tried to break a nail. Leilani had me fucked up.

"Luxe! Please don't leave us!" I heard her crying and screaming, but I needed to teach her ass a lesson. She needed to appreciate a real nigga when she had one. For now, I'm team single, and I don't give a fuck how anyone feels about it. If it's meant to be, then we'll be, and if it's not, I know I did my part by her and Juju. As hard as I just was on Leilani, she has no idea how she fucked me up questioning my love for her. I'm not gonna lie. A nigga kind of hurt, but I'll be okay. The best way to get over a bitch is to get a new one.

Chapter Twelve

Diamond

I had been running around like a chicken with my head cut off getting my grandmother's funeral arrangements together. I hadn't had a moment's rest since I stepped off of the plane. I felt like I was having a setback, because I had literally just given birth; I still have stitches where they made my incision. I had to work through the pain, though, because my grandmother deserved to be put away like the Queen she was. I was more than ready to get back home to my son, though. He was my silver lining in all of the bullshit that was going on.

Since all of the arrangements had been taken care of, I decided to pack up some of my grandmother's effects and have them shipped out to my house and the rest donated to charity. I was packing as much as I could, because my mother was already plotting on selling shit. This bitch really needs to go to rehab. Her mother isn't even in the ground yet, and she's trying to sell her shit. I'm so happy we had been keeping our distance from one another, because I was a second away from kicking her ass like she wasn't my mother.

As I laid in my grandmother's bed, all I could think about was Judah. It was crazy how I loved that man, despite how he'd treated me, and I still love him. After confirming I was indeed pregnant by him, Judah changed for the better. He wasn't putting his hands on me or being disrespectful. He went out of his way to show me how much he loved me and was ready for us to be a family, but then all of a sudden, his mother turned up and changed us. I'm so happy that bitch is dead I don't know what to do, although Judah and I are beefing.

I feel so sorry for him. Judah loved his mother, so finding out how treacherous Ava was had really hurt him. I reached over on the nightstand to call him, but I quickly shut my phone off. I love Judah, but I can't keep letting him make a fool out of me. I just pray he gets his shit together for the sake of our son. I don't want JJ growing up without both of his parents. However, I know I'll be a great single mother to him. I love Judah, but I refuse to subject myself to any more mental or physical abuse at his hands. I don't deserve it.

****

"So when do you think we gonna get the insurance money?" Liz asked as we rode in the family car to the funeral. At the time I was making sure my makeup was fresh; I had been crying all morning, and I was trying my best to make it through the day without crying anymore. I'm sure my grandma wouldn't want me all sad like this.

"Not right now, Liz."

"Liz? Look, Ayanna, or shall I say Diamond. At the end of the of day, I am still your mother. Don't ever call me by my first name. What the hell is wrong with you?" I looked at this bitch like she had lost her mind, because apparently, she did.

"I wish I would call you momma. You've never been a parent to my brothers or me. In case you missed the memo, while you were somewhere sucking dick for a hit, my grandmother raised me. You have never been there for my brothers or me. Had you did your job, Bam would still be here, and Kilo wouldn't be in jail. She fought Cancer for as long as I could remember. Still trying to work while taking Chemo so that we could get what we need. Your ass stressed her out getting high, stealing, and going missing for months at a time.

Please don't come at me crazy about being my mother. My mother has gone onto glory. Please let's get this over with so we don't have to deal with each other. By the way, the rest of the insurance money will go on buying Bam a new headstone and on Kilo's books." This bitch had me fucked up. I swear I wanted to fuck her clean up in the back of this limo, but I knew I couldn't. My grandmother would be so disappointed.

"You think you better than me, don't you? Let me enlighten you daughter of mines. Your ass is not better than me. You think you big shit because you moved out there to Texas and is hugging the pole. Or is it that you think you big shit because you lucked up and met a nigga with money and had a baby with him. Did you forget about your daughter? Well, I didn't. Does your man know about you leaving your little girl at the fire station? Please don't sit here questioning my parenting skills. At least I left you with a family member who I knew would take care you and your brothers. You, on the other hand, abandoned your damn daughter with a note attached. Now she's adopted and being raised by a white family. Miss me with all that shit you talking. We are two of a kind. Like mother and daughter, right?"

I closed my eyes tightly and held in the tears and anger. I've never told anyone about my little girl that I gave up so that she could have a better life. No one knows but my family. I just feel like my life in Chicago is something I left behind. People in Texas didn't need to know what I had been through. I don't want anyone's sympathy.

When I had my daughter, I was thirteen and had no way of taking care of her. At the same time, I couldn't look at the product of rape. One of my brother's closest friends raped me. To this day, I never told Kilo because he was getting in enough trouble, and I knew he would murder him. That's neither here nor there. My daughter is being raised up by a loving family, so I have no regrets. I did it for her, not for me, so fuck Liz and her opinions. If she thought she was gonna get me anymore riled up, then she was sadly mistaken. Fuck Liz.

Shortly after, we made it to the wake, but no one was there. Of course, Liz couldn't sit and just be normal. She didn't even go up to the casket. She quickly rushed out of the funeral home. I didn't know if it was guilt or her ass needed a hit. I started to lightly feel sorry for her, so I placed a kiss on my grandmother's forehead before rushing out to find her. My grandmother looked absolutely beautiful with her good church hat on with the matching outfit. I dressed her in her favorite colors, lavender and white.

"Ms. Brenda always looked good, didn't she?" I quickly turned around, and it was Shawn standing directly behind me. I tried to run, but he grabbed me by my throat and squeezed.

"Let me go!" I barely got out.

"Shut the fuck up! Before I snap your motherfucking neck. Where the fuck is my son at bitch?"

"He's not your son. He's a motherfucking St. Pierre." I kneed him hard as hell in his dick, and he went down like a ton of bricks. All I could do was kick and beat his ass while he was on the floor.

"Get your ass back before I shoot your ass!" He had now upped his gun and was pointing at me. At the same time, people could be heard walking into the chapel.

"This ain't over bitch. I'll be waiting for your bitch ass outside. If you think I'm about to let you be with that bitch ass nigga, Judah, and allow him to raise what's rightfully mines, bitch you crazy. I got our house all set up courtesy of the money I stole from them fuck niggas. By the way, you're late with your payment. I want ten thousand when you walk the fuck out of this funeral, or I'll blast your ass on the Internet and show the world just how you swallow dicks. Don't try no slick shit. I'll be out front. Sorry for your loss."

He slowly backed up and placed the gun behind him as he walked past some of our extended family members. I was scared as fuck, because I knew he would definitely be out front. I needed Judah more than ever right now.

I quickly took my seat with the family, and I tried to make it through the service, but the shit was hard as fuck. I kept looking at the chapel doors to see if Shawn had come back inside. As the preacher alerted us that it was time for the recessional, I became more nervous as I stared back at the doors again. I covered my mouth in shock as I watched my brother Kilo walk down the aisle towards me. He looked so good in all white. His dreads were neatly twisted and hanging down his back. I jumped up and ran towards him fast as hell.

"Kilooooooooooo!!"

"Hey, Lil Sis! I missed your little ass so much." He picked me up and spun me around. For a minute, we just stood, hugging. I was crying so hard on his shoulder.

"Who the fuck is this nigga?" I thought I was hearing shit, but when I looked up, it was Judah.

"Who the fuck is you, nigga?" Kilo pushed me back. Before I could say anything, Judah hit my brother in the jaw. I cringed, because I just knew his shit was broke. Kilo countered and hit Judah's ass right back. It was on from there. They were going blow for blow. The funeral was in complete chaos as people started running for cover watching these fools pull out big ass guns and point them at each other.

"Stop! Judah, this is my brother, Kilo! Kilo, this is Judah, my son's father! Oh my God!" I cried. This was a damn funeral to remember.

"Stop crying. Holla at your boy before he gets fucked up!" Kilo gritted as he put his gun in his waistband.

"Wipe your lip, my nigga, you bleeding," Judah said, smugly, never putting his gun away. I never apologize to any motherfucking body. You're her brother, huh? "Judah looked at me with downcast eyes, because I had never told him anything about me having siblings. This was nothing but another thing added to him not trusting me, but I couldn't worry about that right now. I'll just have to talk to him later; right now, I was more concerned with this nigga Shawn.

"Look, Shawn came in here before the services started and choked me. He threatened me talking about he'll be outside waiting for me." Judah pulled me close and whispered in my ear.

"Finish the services. I'll be outside. Roll with me, Kilo. I got something in my trunk I need to show you." Judah kissed me and walked off like the Boss he was. I prayed to God and my Grandma to forgive me for my sinful thoughts. At the moment, my pussy was dripping like a faucet watching Judah walk out of the chapel. *Yeah, that nigga fucked up about him some Diamond. I wonder what he got in that trunk?*

Chapter Thirteen

Dynasty

It had been a while since I had last graced the club with my presence, and I felt that it was time for me to get back on the scene. Life in the house was boring as hell and this just wasn't for me. I got to give it to Jr., though… he was good company, but I needed to get into the groove of things again. I'm a big girl; I can handle myself. Bitches caught me slipping one time, but that won't be happening again. There wasn't any need for me to be waiting around like a sitting duck for those muthafuckas to come after me when I could be doing something productive with myself. Doing absolutely nothing, but waiting on my men was driving me crazy, and I wanted a piece of the action. Besides, no one had heard a peep from June and Jazzy since all the shit went down, and I wasn't about to keep hiding out like I'm scared of those muthafuckas. Sebastian and everybody else had me fucked up if they thought this was what I was about to keep doing.

Tonight, is the night that we host our monthly Strip-A-Thon, and since Leilani is out of commission due to her having to take care of Juju, I'll just have to take her place. The show must go on, and the money still must be made. Money shortages is a no-no for boss bitches. Not feeling comfortable enough to leave the boys with the nanny or Sebastian's goons, I called up Leilani to see if she would watch the kids. Once she confirmed that she would, I asked Griselda to get them dressed and then returned to my room to do the same. Since I'm the boss for tonight, and dancing wasn't on my agenda, I pulled out my black Prada pants suit from the closet; I had been waiting to wear that baby. Afterwards, I headed for the restroom to get myself together.

As I stood in the mirror observing myself, I couldn't help but smile at how good I looked. Underneath my opened blazer, I wore a black corset that had my breasts sitting upright. My aqua blue hair, which had been freshly dyed, was placed in a bun at the top of my head, and my face was beat, and yes, it was by the gods. Since there was still some bruising on my face, I wore a little more makeup than I usually would, but it was tasteful. After spraying myself with Gucci Guilty for women, I slid my feet into my red Louboutin pumps, grabbed my red clutch, and then exited the room. I had Sebastian's thugs to load the boys in the car and then off to Leilani's we went.

****

"Hey, girl! You look real cute," Leilani cheerfully greeted, as she opened the door and snatched Lil Judah's car seat from my hands.

"Thanks, girl," I replied, and followed her inside. "You sure it's okay to leave the boys? I know you got a lot to do with Juju. I can take them back with me if you want me to."

She waved me off, "Yes, girl. I'm fine; Juju is gonna be happy to have somebody else to play with."

Luxe's home was nice as hell, and I don't think I had really paid it any attention the last time we were here. His shit, like Sebastian's, was a damn mini-mansion, and he had it decked to the nines. Those niggas were getting crazy paper, and you could definitely tell.

Once we entered Juju's room, I rushed to his bed, and placed a kiss on his forehead, "Hey baby; Auntie has been missing you sooooo much."

He smiled as he looked at me all bright eyed, "I missed you, too. Are you staying with me for a while?"

"Nah, baby; I got to go take care of some business, but I'll be back over here to chill with you tomorrow. Is that okay?"

He nodded his head, "It's okay, but only if you bring me something back."

Leilani's head whipped in his direction, "Juju, you don't need shit else so stop begging."

I chuckled because he was always pimping me, but she was getting in our business, and she knew better. Whatever Juju wants, Juju gets, and I'm tired of having to tell her that.

"Back off, heifer; this is an a and b conversation."

"So see your way out." Juju finished, and we high-fived.

"Don't get yo ass whooped." Leilani threatened.

"You ain't whooping shit." I kissed Juju's forehead and whispered in his ear. "I got you; yo momma don't run shit."

"I heard you." Leilani intervened.

I waved her off and kissed the boys once more, "I'm about to go y'all so be good and see you later girl. I'll be here first thing in the morning, Leilani."

"Alright, have dumb and dumber lock the door behind you."

****

It was seven-thirty when I made it to the club, and there were very few patrons scattered about. Getting straight to business, I headed for Leilani's office and grabbed her checklist of things to do from her vision board. That girl was always on top of things when it came to running shit, so I knew she'd have everything mapped out for me, and I wouldn't have to fret. After making sure that everything was in place and the girls had everything they needed, I retreated to the office to kick back before the doors opened; being the boss was hard work, but I was enjoying every moment of it. It made me think further about what I really wanted to do with my life.

"Knock, knock," Sebastian stated before he opened the door and stepped inside.

I rolled my eyes, "What's up? Don't come in here with no bullshit. I don't have time for it right now. I'm having a peaceful day, and I want it to remain that way."

With an agitated expression on his face, he rushed behind the desk where I sat and snatched me from the seat,

"I'm sick of you and this bitch ass attitude. What did I tell you was gone happen if you keep on?"

I heard what he said, but snatching me up was a no, no, so I looked down at his hands, and then to his face.

"Get yo nasty ass hands off me before we rumble in this bitch." I threatened.

"Oh, we about to rumble alright." He replied, and then roughly flipped me around.

With one hand, he pushed me forward onto the desk and with the other, he snapped the button on my pants, and then snatched them down. With all my might, I tried to raise up but I was no match for his strength, and he wasn't letting up. While I struggled with his weight, he violently kicked my legs apart and then snatched my thong off, leaving me fully exposed. As the cold air whisked over my hot spot, immediately, my clit started throbbing, and my breathing picked up. Looking back at him, I eyed him sexily, and he licked his lips lustfully before he smacked my ass.

"You my bitch and you gonna have to put some respect on my name."

He unzipped his pants and let them fall to the floor.

"Fuck you! I'm not your bitch! I'm bout to get me a new nigga." I replied, through deep, raspy, breaths.

With one hand, he smacked my kitty with his hardened wood, grabbed me around my neck with the other, and then lifted me to where my back was against his chest.

"Bitch, you better quit playing with me." He warned, before thrusting himself inside my slippery slope.

I inhaled, deeply, and my tongue hung out as I panted like a dog in heat. With each rhythmic thrust, I could feel Sebastian digging deeper and deeper into my guts. It had been a minute since we explored each other's bodies, and that shit was feeling good as hell.

"Shit, Daddy," I moaned, while rolling my hips to match his rhythm.

He squeezed my neck a little tighter as his warm breath brushed against my ear.

"Oh, I'm Daddy now, huh." He replied, tauntingly. "Okay, since I'm Daddy, why don't you come on this dick for me."

"I'm not ready," I grunted, defiantly.

Hearing that must've pissed him off, because he released my neck and threw me forward onto the desk once again. With both hands, he spread my cheeks and held them open while he plowed into me.

"You gonna learn about being hard headed. I'm the mutha fucking man in this relationship."

Grinding into him harder than before, I closed my eyes and reveled in the feeling that he was giving me. It wasn't until I felt that tingling sensation in my stomach that I realized just how much I missed him.

"Come on this dick." He demanded, once again, and my legs started shaking.

Nodding my head, I bit down on my lips as waves of exotic pleasures rocked my body and went sliding down his wood.

"I'm… coming." I screamed.

He placed his hand over my mouth, "Shhh, be quiet girl. We not at home."

I didn't give a fuck where we were; this nigga had me gone, so it was what it was. In the short time that we had been together, he had learned my body and knew how to make it succumb to him, whether I wanted it to or not. As mad as I had been with him, once he entered me, those feelings started dwindling with each tap of my spot.

"It's your turn." I lifted one leg and planted it on the desk. With my ass in the air, I lay my breasts flat on the desk, gave my back a deep arch, and smacked my own ass." "Get this pussy, Daddy," I demanded.

With that, he roughly gripped my waist and slammed me down on his dick. My eyes rolled into the back of my head, and I bit my lip so hard that the metallic taste of blood filled my mouth.

"This what you want?" he asked, and I nodded my head.

"Don't shake yo head, answer me." He roared, as he punished my pussy some more.

"Yes, Daddy, yes." I moaned, while taking his pipe like a big girl.

His thrusts became deeper, and I could feel him getting even harder than before. As I squeezed his member with my walls, he grunted louder and slightly lowered himself onto my back. Sweat beads rolled from his forehead, and he nibbled on my ear.

"I'm bout to shoot this load in you."

Hearing that shit pissed me off; was this nigga trying to trap me? As before, I tried to raise up, but with his weight being on me, it was damn near impossible.

"You bet not nut in me, Sebastian; I'm not playing with you."

He grunted as he squeezed his eyes shut, "It's… too… late! Argh!"

His body convulsed as his throbbing wood pulsated against my walls, and he collapsed putting all of his weight on my back. Pissed, I bowed him in his ribs, and he chuckled as he lifted himself.

"Ouch, fuck you do that for?"

With a mug on my face, I lifted myself from the desk and turned to face him, "I told you not to fucking nut in me. If I get pregnant against my will, I just want you to know I'm not having it."

His pupils glazed over and his cheeks turned purple in color as he violently grabbed me around my neck and lifted me into the air while squeezing it tighter than he ever had before.

"If you play with me about my seed, I'm gone kill you, and I promise you that." He threatened, in a way that he never had.

After lowering me back to my feet, I held my hands around my neck while trying to catch my breath. To be quite frank, I had never seen him get that way before, and it frightened me but turned me on at the same time. Snatching me up, he threw my back against the wall and looked down into my eyes. With his chest pressed against mine, he all but growled.

"Did you fucking understand me?" I quickly nodded my head yes. "Good, now get yourself cleaned up and come downstairs. People will be piling inside in a few minutes. You need to be out there to greet them."

"Okay," I replied, lowly.

"Okay, what?"

"Okay, Daddy." I purred.

"Let me spit some real shit to you, Dynasty. I know that you all independent and don't like to take orders and shit. At the same time, no matter what the fuck you do or say, I'm the motherfucking man in this relationship. I slang cock, and you take it. Stop walking around here acting like you can whoop my ass. I let you get away with that shit in the car, but you starting to take shit too far. Your feistiness is one of the things I love about you. At the same time, that shit is becoming a fucking turn-off. You need to know when to speak and when to shut the fuck up. Stay in your lane, and act like a fucking lady.

All this rah-rah shit you be on is unladylike, and it's pissing me off. You're far too fucking beautiful to have such a nasty ass attitude. Learn to submit every once in a while and just follow my lead. You need to calm your ass down with all this gun slinging shit you be on, too. I'm the man in this relationship. I'll hold court in the streets, and you hold down the home front. You can stop rolling your motherfucking eyes, too, and getting loud with me. That shit is so disrespectful. Tighten up before I fuck you up!"

He fixed his clothes and then pecked my lips before slowly backing away with his eyes trained on me. I guess he figured I was gonna try to go after him, but I was too turned on for all of that. Still slightly shocked by the way he handled me, I watched intently as he exited the room and closed the door behind him. I shook my head; that man was something else. In less than thirty minutes, he trotted into the office, fucked the shit out of me, choked the hell out of me, put me in check, and made me fall even more in love with him than before. Damn, I'm a sucker for love.

Just like Sebastian told me to, I cleaned myself up and got ready to head downstairs. It took me longer than expected, because he had drained the hell out of me. It wasn't until I looked out the glass window that exposed the bottom floor, that I notice how the club had gotten thick as hell, and I needed to be getting on out there.

Before stepping out, I stopped by the window once more to get a good look at all the people who were out to kick it with us, and just when I was about to exit, I had to stop and double back because some new niggas caught my attention. A sexy, red ass nigga was leading the pack, and his swag caught all my attention. *He can get it.* I thought to myself while straightening my jacket to go and greet them first. Behind him, about ten dudes filed; however, they all went their separate ways and that raised my suspicions. Clearly, I could tell they were together, because the leader was trying to discreetly give orders without bringing too much attention to them. I watched intensely as some scattered towards the right and some dispersed towards the left, strategically stopping in places that had them surrounding the club. That was odd, but remembering what Sebastian had just said, I tried not to pay it much mind. Maybe, just maybe, I was a tad bit paranoid, because of all that happened, but deep down, my intuition was telling me something was about to happen.

Pushing my paranoia to the back, I continued watching and nothing else seemed to be out of order. That is… until I saw June pull up from the rear and whisper something in the sexy one's ear.

I know this nigga got to know this is our shit, so seeing him meant nothing but trouble. After removing the safety latch on my gun that I had on my waist, I ran to my bag and grabbed my other pistol. I didn't know what this nigga had up, but I wasn't waiting around to see. It was about to be on and popping.

Chapter Fourteen

Sebastian

After my encounter with Dynasty's crazy ass, I rushed to the bar because I needed a stiff drink. She knew exactly what to do to work a nigga's nerves to the max, but despite that, she was still my baby. I know breaking her down won't be easy, but I love a challenge, so it was going to be okay. Once we get back on one accord, shit is gonna go smoothly; I'll deal with whatever I have to, for now.

"Let me get a Remy on the rocks," I instructed the bartender and then turned around to face the rowdy crowd.

"Here you go, Mr. St. Pierre." The bartender slid me my drink, and I took a sip.

"I see you gave me a double…"

She anxiously pointed behind me with her mouth hanging open interrupting me before I could finish my statement.

"What the fuck is wrong with ya girl? Look." She pointed again.

Quickly snapping my head in the direction of the stairs, time seemed to have slowed as I watched Dynasty rapidly descend the steps with a devilish look on her face and her guns aimed at someone in the crowd. I didn't know exactly what the fuck was going on, and I honestly didn't need to. If her guns were about to blaze, then so were mine. It was about to be me and my girlfriend on some ninety-six Bonnie and Clyde type shit. After removing the pistols from my back, I downed the rest of my drink, slammed my glass on the bar, and began violently pushing through the crowd.

Bok, bok, bok!

Shots fired, and then, the next thing I knew, bullets started flying from every angle. From that point on, I was on go mode, and I was gonna murder everything moving that I felt like was a threat.

Trying to get out the way of all the chaos, most patrons immediately ran towards the exit, while the others did the smart thing and dropped to the floor, all trying to get out the line of fire. As I frantically bowed my way through the sea of people to get to my girl, I spotted a dude with his guns pointed at Dynasty, and I wasted no mutha fucking time to make my move. With absolutely no emotions, I bodied that bitch ass nigga by sending two shots to the dome. After taking care of him, my eyes were alert and attentive, as I scanned the club for unfamiliar faces, and each time I spotted one, they were firing their pistol towards my lady. These niggas had to know she wasn't by herself.

"You bitch ass niggas violated when you came in my club with this hoe shit," She screamed while sending bullets their way. "I'mma kill all you fuck niggas!"

One of the dude's back was to me, as I frantically made my way up the right side; he wasn't watching his

114

surroundings. If he had been, he would've been able to see me easing up behind him. Too bad for him, though; he had fucked up, and now it was gonna cost him his life. Noticing that he had a good shot on Dynasty, I placed my gun on the back of his head, and my finger lightly grazed the trigger, causing his head to bust wide open like a watermelon.

At the same time, we were both coming up opposite sides, guns barking. Bumping into her, I jumped, because I didn't know who it was, and we both turned our guns on each other before realizing who the other one was. Finally together, we stood back to back in the center of the dancefloor, dropping anybody coming our way. Those niggas must don't know we had mad love in these streets, because not only did they have to worry about us, they had to worry about some of the other crews, and my bouncers that were bussing, too. Seeing that they were outnumbered, I watched them as they started backing out.

Dynasty was amped, and there was nothing I could do to calm her down as she chased those fuck boys out the door. Running behind her, I snatched her ass up in the air and briskly whisked her away before she got herself hurt. While she kicked, screamed, and talked shit, I carried her ass right back inside. That was the same shit we had just talked about, and she was pissing me off.

"What the fuck was you thinking, Dynasty?" I asked, as I placed her on her feet.

"I wasn't thinking! I was after June, and I would've had him if you didn't grab me." She paced back and forth.

"June? I didn't see June."

"Why the fuck do you think I was bussin? Them muthafuckas came in here to fuck some shit up. I wasn't having that."

"Damn that, you need to warn me if you see shit popping off before I do."

She shook her head, "Wasn't no time for that. It was time to go."

If I never wanted to smack the taste out of her mouth, right then was it, but I thought better of it when I saw her scratch the side of her head with her gun.

"Look, you go ahead and leave. I'mma wait here for the police so we can get this shit straight."

"Speaking of police, here. Write this number down."

"What number?"

"The license plate number on the truck I was chasing. I was able to remember it and that it had New York plates."

Shaking my head to the side, I had to chuckle; Dynasty never ceases to amaze me.

Chapter Fifteen

Leilani

It had been three days and four nights since Luxe had left the house, and he hadn't been back since. Yea, I know he was mad at me for questioning his motives, but that shit he doing is crazy. With all that's going on, why the fuck would he think that it's cool for him to stay away. My feelings were just all over the place; there had been too many things happening in the short amount of time that we'd been together. Furthermore, if it were something that I would have done on my part, he would've been thinking the same thing.

While pacing back and forth, I snatched my phone from my pocket, dialed his number, and waited for him to answer. I needed to at least hear his voice.

"What?" he answered, unpleasantly.

"Don't fucking what me, Luxe! Where the hell are you?" I sobbed.

He sucked his teeth, "Don't be asking me no questions about nothing. I thought it was understood where we stand before I left."

"Look, I know you mad and all, but damn. How you just gonna leave us here by ourselves? I thought the purpose of you bringing me here was so you could watch over us.

You; not your damn goons. I'm sorry, baby. Please just come home. We miss you." I begged although I didn't feel that I should've had too.

"I'll be there later." Luxe replied, roughly, and then hung up in my face.

Sobbing loudly, I threw my body on the bed and placed my face in the crook of my arm. I was hurting and didn't know what I could do to make Luxe forgive me. Deep down, I believed he really loved me, but I was too mad to see that. However, I see it now, and I want to show him how much, but now he's doing hurtful shit, and I don't know how much I can take.

"What the fuck is wrong with you?" Dynasty asked as she burst into my room.

I stood from the bed, ran over to her, and threw my arms around her shoulders; I needed my friend's comfort right about now. It was mid-afternoon, and she was supposed to have already been here, but I knew she wasn't coming early in the morning like she said. I wasn't tripping, though, because she couldn't have come at a better time.

With tears, and snot running down my nose, I wiped my face with my sleeve and then replied, "It's Luxe; he hasn't been home in days, and that shit got me going crazy."

"Nah bitch, wipe yo face, because we about to turn the fuck up. That's one of the reasons I came in here. I got to show you something, and I need to tell you about what happened at the club last night." She pulled her phone from her back pocket.

"Don't worry about telling me about what happened at the club, because I already know. I'm just glad everyone is okay. What? What you got to show me, though?" I asked her, heart now pounding out of my chest.

She placed the phone in my hand, "So before I got out the bed this morning, I was scrolling down Instagram and saw a picture of Luxe in this hoe bed sleep. Where the fuck they do that at?"

As I examined the picture closely, my mood shifted from hurt to pissed. Here I was crying over this nigga, and he somewhere laid up with a bitch.

"Ohh bitch, when I find him, I'mma fuck his ass up! He don't even fucking know who he playing with."

Dynasty smiled, wickedly, "Oh there's no need to find him. I know exactly where that bitch stays, so put on some clothes and let's fucking go."

"How the fuck you know where that bitch stay?"

Dynasty frowned at me, "Bitch, don't look at me accusingly. The only reason I have any idea where the hoe stays is because she lives by my Grandma. She one of the old hoes that used to be hitting on my brother. I had to check the hoe a time or two."

"Oh, okay," I replied, approvingly.

"Bitch, oh okay nothing. Just hurry the fuck up,"

She didn't have to say shit but a word, because I ran to that closet so damn quick it was unreal. I threw on a lime green and black Nike tight set with my Air Forces to match, threw my hair in a ponytail, grabbed my keys, and headed out the room with Dynasty on my heels. After giving the Nanny strict instructions, we both ran out the front door.

****

A few minutes later, we pulled alongside the curb right in front of the bitch's house. Before exiting the car, I popped the trunk and removed my bat.

"Nah, bitch! Put that muthafucking bat down. This Luxe we dealing with; here." She handed me one of her guns.

I couldn't do nothing but shake my head; Dynasty was gonna have me catching a murder case. Before approaching the house, I had to make sure the coast was clear. Despite me having Gangsta Boo with me, I wasn't tryna catch no cases. From the outside, we could hear R. Kelly as he blasted from the speakers inside the house, and I got even madder. With my hand gripped firmly around the handle of the pistol, Dynasty and I briskly walked side by side up the sidewalk. Once we climbed the steps onto the porch, I raised my hand to knock on the door, but again, Dynasty stopped me.

"What the fuck are you doing? Don't be knocking on this hoe door. We are on a gangsta muthafucka mission. Kick that bitch in!"

"Nah Dynasty, you trippin!"

She looked at me like I had two heads, "Nah bitch, I'm not the one tripping. The one trippin is Luxe. Ain't no muthafuckin way he supposed to be laid up with no bullshit ass bitch. Fuck him; he probably raw dogged. You know they don't like using rubbers."

Hearing that really pissed me the fuck off, and that was all it took for me to kick that door with all my fucking might. However, I wasn't strong enough to do it by myself, and Dynasty saw that.

"Come on, we gone kick it together, ole weak ass." She joked. "I'm glad that damn music is up that loud, because if not, you would've got us busted."

I waved her off, "On the count of three. One… two… three."

On cue, we kicked the door and filed inside, ready to take they heads off.

Dynasty tapped my shoulder and pointed up, "The music is coming from upstairs, so that's probably where they at. Come on."

My feet were heavy as hell, as I walked up the steps behind Dynasty, and I almost wanted to turn around for fear of what I might see going on. If Luxe was upstairs fucking a bitch after I just begged him to come home, I was going to go ape shit on both of them.

Dynasty stopped outside the door, "Here is where the music coming from. I would go in, but this yo nigga so, I'mma leave the honors up to you."

121

I nibbled the inside of my jaw nervously, "I don't know if I can do this. I'm scared of what I might do."

"Fuck that! We didn't come all the way over here for nothing. Bitch, we going inside so bring yo ass on."

Slowly, I inhaled deep breaths to calm myself before the storm that laid brewing inside me came to fruition. My face wrinkled into a demon-like statue, my palms were sweaty, and my heart beat rapidly. Visions of me pounding Luxe's head in with the pistol was hyping me up. Adrenaline shot straight to my brain, giving me a euphoric feeling of power, and I was ready to tear his ass to pieces.

As I entered the room, I noticed their clothes were scattered across the floor, as if they had torn them off of each other. The room was dimly lit, and there were candles all over. I tiptoed my way in that direction with Dynasty on my heels. Luxe was lying on his back, naked as the day he was born, and I noticed his limp pole was sticky. Thinking back to what Dynasty said about him not using a condom, I became infuriated.

Pissed, I grabbed the empty bottle of Hennessy and smashed it on the wall by the top of their head, but he didn't move. However, the chic did, and Dynasty put her pistol in her face to shut her the fuck up. I threw the bottle to the side; fuck that, I didn't want to cut him. I wanted to shoot his ass

"Wake yo bitch ass up, nigga," I stated, forcefully, as I tapped the center of his forehead with my gun.

Hearing my voice made his eyes pop open, and he quickly sat up in bed, while staring down the barrel of the gun.

After realizing it was me who had caught him slipping, he raised his hands in the air. "Baby, it's not what it looks like."

"Yes, it is bitch," I interrupted before he got to tell any more lies.

Seeing the look on his face pissed me off even more so I threw the gun to the side and dived on top of his ass, reigning blows. Following my lead, Dynasty placed her gun in the back of her pants and lifted the bitch from the bed by her hair and went to beating the shit outta her. He was gone learn about playing with me.

Chapter Sixteen

Luxe

A nigga was completely caught off guard with this shit here. For a minute, I was so out of it that I didn't really realize what the fuck was going on until I saw Leilani standing over me. Staring down the barrel of her gun had a both nigga scared and pissed off at the same motherfucking time. The fact that this bitch had really put a gun to my head like I was some type of hoe ass nigga had crossed some major ass boundaries with me.

The Hennessy I had been drinking and the Kush I was smoking had clouded my judgment. It was never my intention to end up staying the night with Monae. There was nothing between us at all. A bitch was the last thing on my mind. I had major shit going on in the streets, and I needed to be focused. Monae was a slut I had been fucking with from time to time over the years. Since I had got with Leilani and made shit official, I hadn't even thought about another bitch. I was honestly ready for forever with her, but just knowing that she doubted my intentions with her had me questioning everything.

I was at the club when I ran into Monae, and we caught up with each other over casual conversation. One thing led to another, and that's how I ended up back at her crib. I was so wasted that I don't remember shit; I had got caught slipping in a major way. Once I gathered myself, I jumped up and threw on my clothes. A nigga was asshole naked with dick hanging everywhere, too. I was trying my best to get control of the situation, but I was no match for both Leilani and Dynasty together. However, since Leilani couldn't get at me like she wanted to, she settled with going after Monae, and they were fucking her up. I felt bad for Monae, because she had no win with these motherfuckers. I watched Dynasty hit her across the face with her gun, and blood instantly squirted out of it.

"That's enough! Break this shit up!"

"Do you love this bitch, Luxe?" Leilani asked, while punching Monae in the mouth one more time.

Shaking my head at Leilani, I decided to tell the truth, "Nah, I don't love her, but I do have love for her, as in a friendship type of way. We've been knowing each other for years."

"Oh, so you got love for this bitch, huh," she cocked her gun. "Well Luxe, do you love this bitch to death?" Leilani challenged, as she walked towards me with a pistol in her hand.

"What the fuck is you talking about Leilani? I'm trying to stop y'all from killing the motherfucking girl. Your ass better pipe the fuck down while you're walking towards me with that gun." I threatened, getting more and more pissed off by the second.

"You taking up for this bitch!" Leilani swung on me and cracked my ass in the jaw. I didn't mean to do it, but my reflexes made me draw back and slap the fuck out of her, and that made her drop the gun. From that point on, we continued to tussle.

"Oh, hell no! You ain't about to be putting your hands on her!" Dynasty had screamed before she came at me like a raging bull.

I couldn't believe these crazy bitches had beat Monae unconscious and were now fighting me. They both had me fucked up. I managed to quickly pick up the gun that Leilani had dropped. At the same, I started backing out of the bedroom and down the stairs. I was trying to get the fuck out of there before I fucked around and killed one of their asses.

"Get the fuck back!" I said, as I aimed my gun at their ass.

"Really, Luxe!" Leilani cried, as she continued to walk towards me. Had this been any other time, I would have been more sympathetic. However, I wasn't. I wanted to beat her ass for her behavior this morning. Just looking at Dynasty carrying on, I knew she was behind Leilani doing this; this crazy shit had her name written all over it. It was one thing for Dynasty to act all ghetto and shit, but another when Leilani acts ghetto. I'm not feeling that shit at all. Leilani is a motherfucking boss, and this shit is so beneath her. Hell, it's beneath Dynasty, but ain't no reasoning with her.

"Yeah, really!" I said, as I backed out of the door. At first, I was about to leave both of them crazy bitches, but then I thought about it, and Leilani was taking her ass home with me. She shouldn't be out of the fucking house anyway. Glancing over in Dynasty's direction, I noticed this crazy bitch was still walking up on me like I wasn't aiming a gun at her ass. Shaking my damn head, I swear this bitch was going to make me shoot her crazy ass; I don't know how my brother do it. I swear, if it were me, I would body this lunatic bitch. I love my Sis, but her ass is too fucking nutty for me.

"I am not Sebastian. I will shoot your motherfucking ass! Leilani, get the fuck in the car, and I'm not going to tell you again." I was tired of playing with Dynasty and Leilani's ass.

"Really Luxe? You would shoot a lady." Dynasty said with an evil grin.

"Hell yeah, I would shoot your ass. You ain't no lady. You're a nigga with a pussy!"

"Yeah aight!! Bitch don't get in that car with him!" Dynasty tried to stop Leilani.

POW!!

"I'm not playing with your crazy ass, Dynasty. Get the fuck back. I won't miss next time. Bring your ass on right now!" I grabbed Leilani by the back of the neck and pushed her towards my car with so much force she almost fell and busted her shit. She got me fucked up, but I got her, though. If she wants to put guns to my head and fight; I'm going to give her that. I'm all about that gunplay and throwing these hands.

"You better not hurt my friend, Luxe. I'm not playing with you." Dynasty yelled out, and I quickly pulled off without even responding to her ass.

"I don't know why you're over there crying. Man the fuck up! You just put a motherfucking gun to my head like you don't know who the hell I am!"

I hit the steering wheel over and over again. I swear to God I was hot with Leilani. I legit wanted to do her in for the disrespect.

"I don't know who the fuck you think you are, nigga. In case you forgot, I just found you naked in bed with another bitch. You're the same one who pulled a gun on me like you don't know who the fuck I am. So, don't go getting all in your feelings like you ain't did shit to me! I can't believe you cheated on me, motherfucker!" Leilani reached over and slapped the shit out of me, and following that, she straddling me and was trying to claw my eyes. I couldn't even hit her ass back, because I was trying to steer the car and keep us from crashing.

"Stop, Leilani! Before you kill both of us."

"I don't give a fuck, Luxe! You fucked that bitch, and I want to kill your ass."

I finally was able to look around her so I could pull over to the side of the road. With force, I pushed her ass off of me, and she landed in the passenger seat.

"You want to fight, huh?" I said looking into the rearview mirror. My face was scratched up, and it looked like my damn eye was swelling.

"Hell, yeah. I want to fight your ass!"

"Say no more." I did a U-Turn in the middle of the street and headed to my office. We rode in silence for the next ten minutes until we pulled up and hopped out. I walked around to the passenger's side and yanked the door open.

"Don't touch me, Luxe! Take me home. I'm good on your ass."

"Nah! Ain't no going home. You want to fight right? Well, let's do this shit the right way. Follow me." I pulled her ass out and basically dragged her ass into the building and downstairs to the basement. Grabbing a set a boxing gloves, I threw them at her.

"What the fuck are these for?"

"Let's rock. You said you want to fight, right?" I placed my gloves on my hand and squared up with her ass. She had tears streaming down her face, and I was starting to feel fucked up, because I didn't want to hurt Leilani anymore than I already had. I just couldn't deal with her feeling like it was okay to put a gun to my head. The worse part about all of this was the fact that I had to put my hands on her. I'm not that type of a nigga.

"I'm tired of fighting, Luxe. I literally don't have any more fight in me. All I got in this life is my son. He's the only one I can depend on; every man I have loved has broken my heart. At least, I know that he won't."

Hearing that, I dropped the gloves I had in my hand and pulled her close.

"All I can say is that I'm sorry you had to see me like that. I haven't been with another bitch since we made shit official. I know that don't make it right, so I won't stand here and make an excuse as to why I fucked the bitch. I'm just not that type of nigga. At the same time, I told you where the fuck we stood when you assassinated my motherfucking character. I fucked the bitch, and it's nothing I can do about that now. At this point, it's only two things we can do; we can move on and fix this shit, or we can say fuck it and walk away. The last thing I want to do is ever cause you any pain. I love you and Ju-Ju more than anything in this world, but what I won't do is kiss your ass to try and convince you of this."

"After seeing you in bed with another woman, I know I don't want us anymore. That shit showed me that, when shit gets hectic, you find comfort in others instead of coming home and fixing it. Four days you left me and Ju-Ju in the house like our lives wasn't in danger. I don't ask for much, Luxe, but I deserved better than to be abandoned for questioning your intentions. You were supposed to understand my position on the matter. After all, you played a big part in it whether you want to take ownership of the issue or not. It's cool, Luxe; no hard feelings. Please just get me to the house so I can get my things. I'm moving back into my home; I feel like it's for the better."

I ran my hand over my face in frustration listening to Leilani; I had been through more than enough for one day. Just like she was tired of fighting, I was sick of trying to show her ass that I love her. If being out of this shit with a nigga is what she wanted then who was I to make her stay?

"That's cool." I agreed with her, because I've never been the type of nigga that tried to keep a bitch that didn't want to stay.

Do I love her ... Yes. Will I sweat her to be with me... No. Besides her catching me cheating, I've always been good to Leilani and Ju-Ju. He and I have formed a bond, and it hurts to know it's so easy for her to just take him from me. Right now, I was regretting going against everything I've stood for to be with her. Luxe St. Pierre doesn't fall in love; fuck Leilani!

Chapter Seventeen

Judah

I thought I was seeing shit when I pulled up and saw this nigga Shawn leaning against a car. Before making any moves, I looked around to peep the scenery to see how in the fuck I was going to get at dude. It was broad daylight so I knew I couldn't just shoot his ass. I could tell by where he was positioned that he was trying not to be seen, so I bussed a couple of blocks to check everything out before I made my move. There was no way in hell I was letting him get away after what the fuck he did. I was also pissed at the fact that he was in a close proximity of Diamond. That shit was no coincidence.

After bussing one last block, I finally saw that everything was clear so I decided to go ahead and snatch Shawn's ass up. It was at the right time, too, because he was so into his phone conversation that he snoozed and fucked around and got caught slipping. Sneaking up from the rear, I punched that nigga in the back of the head so hard he blacked out, and I quickly scooped his ass up and put him in my trunk. After that, I looked around to make sure the coast was still clear and then casually headed to the funeral home.

Man, seeing Diamond hugged up with that dread head ass nigga sent me over the edge. I didn't think about asking any questions; I just wanted to fuck him up for even being so close to her. My actions alone showed me that I was more in love with Diamond than I believed. I could never see myself being all emotional over no bitch, but she had me acting real nutty behind her ass.

I could hear the fear in Diamond's voice as she told me about Shawn's bitch ass. The fact that she was scared of this nigga had me hot. My girl ain't never got to be scared of no nigga; I don't even want her to be afraid of me. For him putting fear in her heart alone… he had to die. That, accompanied with the fact that he had stolen money from me and was extorting Diamond, and I couldn't wait to make this motherfucker a distant memory.

******

"So what's your beef with this nigga?" Kilo asked.

"He stole a lot of money from me and my brothers. I've been looking for this motherfucker for a minute." I replied, while cutting the chainsaw on, then slicing his ass across the chest. I then passed it to Kilo.

"Ahhhhhhh!" Shawn screamed.

"Shut your bitch ass up! Was you doing all that shit when you was fucking with my sister? Where the motherfucking pictures and videos at nigga?" Kilo asked, as he walked around and sliced Shawn across the back.

134

"Ahhhhhhh! The files are in my phone in the email" He managed to yell.

"Yo, Diamond!" I called up the stairs.

With all the drama that kicked off, the family refused to come to the repast that Diamond had put together. Since we had nowhere else to take Shawn, we brought him here.

"Huh?"

"Come down here for a minute!"

"No, Judah. I can't look at him."

"Bring your ass down here, Diamond!" I didn't mean to raise my voice, but I didn't like that shakiness in hers when she replied.

I needed to get her out of that shit for real. I didn't like Dynasty's behavior, but she's all good for bullshit and down to ride for my brother, and I needed Diamond to be the same damn way. Even though, somewhere along the way, I think Sebastian handed Dynasty his balls.

"What, Judah?"

"Grab them garden shears and come over here?" Shawn began to thrash around, and I gestured for Kilo to come over and help me hold his ass in place.

"Really, nigga? You about to put her in this shit." Kilo asked.

"Hell yeah. This bitch ass nigga been fucking with Diamond and got her all scared and shit. This shit is so much bigger than him stealing money from me. His bitch ass crossed the line extorting her. Threatening her and shit with them damn photos and videos. So, yeah I'm putting her in this shit. It's only right she gets at that nigga.

"I'm okay, Judah. Just go ahead and kill him. I'm ready to get back home to Dallas. I miss JJ." She wiped her face, and I could tell that she was upset.

As bad as I wanted her to watch, and help, me kill this nigga, I knew she needed me more.
"Okay. Go upstairs and wait for me."

Without another word, she turned around and headed back out the way she came.

"Maybe I should go up there and check on my Sis. I've been away so long, and Diamond has grown up on a nigga. I can't even believe she's a mother. Her and our grandmother were close as hell, so I know she going through it right now. I just want to say thanks for looking out for her. She didn't have anyone while I was down. Our brother Bam got murked right before I went away, and our OG been strung out all of our lives. She needed someone to take care of her for a change. That stripping shit was not cool. She's tried to keep it a secret from me, but I found out when I was locked up."

Just hearing him speak on their life made me feel like shit. I had never taken the time to sit back and think about where she came from and how she ended up stripping. It was fucked up that I didn't even know she had brothers. It fucked with me in a way to know that she didn't feel like she could open up to me. Obviously, she had her reasons so I wouldn't press the issue.

"Look, I need you to finish this nigga while I get Diamond over to the hotel. I'll book you a room as well. I'm staying at the Trump Towers. I'll leave some cash and your key card at the front desk. When you make it over there, you can scoop her and have a sit-down. You guys need that time to catch up; It's been a minute. We need to have one as well; I know that you're fresh out and you look like you can put in work. I have some shit back home in Dallas for you. I'll give you some time to think about it. In the meantime, take this nigga out of his misery. Bitch ass nigga not even a fun kill. He don't talk shit or beg for his life." I reached inside of the nigga's pocket and grabbed his phone before heading upstairs to scoop Diamond.

******

It had been about two hours since we had made it to my hotel. Diamond had yet to utter a word to me. The most I heard her voice was when she was on FaceTime with Dynasty. I peeked in the room and watched as she talked to our son, and I could tell that she was so in love him. Her face lit up when she spoke baby talk to him. I don't know what's going on, but it's like the blinders I had on my eyes were slowly being removed. I was seeing Diamond differently.

As I sat in the living room area of our suite, I nursed some Remy and smoked some Kush. I was becoming uneasy, because neither one of my brothers were answering their phones. That shit was absolutely frustrating. I guess they were fine, because Diamond hadn't told me anything different. She had been on the phone with Dynasty and Leilani, and I knew they were bashing the hell out of me and my brothers.

It was as if she was hiding in the bedroom. I had been trying to give her the space that she apparently wanted, but I didn't fly all the way out here for us to ignore one another. Granted, we weren't on the best of terms when she left, but I was ready to fix it. I just wasn't sure that she was. I decided to stop waiting for her to make the first move. The hardcore ass nigga inside of me was blocking me from that part of me that wanted to be happy. I was raised not to fall in love, so when I did, I fought the shit strictly because I didn't know how to handle it. I got up and headed towards the room, but I stopped when I heard them talking over the speaker phone.

"Judah don't love me, Lani. It feels like he never loved me. Getting pregnant with JJ was merely a mistake on his part. I feel like, had I not got pregnant, he never would have fucked with me. To him, I'm nothing but some stripper bitch that does tricks for a living."

"Don't say that, Diamond. You're so much more than that. Trust me, Judah loves you. It's just that the way they were raised makes them insensitive to women. It's not that he doesn't care about you; Judah just doesn't know how. Look, I got to go; somebody at the door. Stop crying. I love you, Sis."

Damn! I thought to myself. The last thing I wanted was her to think was that I didn't love her at all. I walked into of the room and sat down on the bed, so she got up and tried to rush into the bathroom, but I quickly stood up and pulled her back to me.

"Where you going?"

"I have to use the bathroom, Judah." She replied, looking down at the floor, so I lifted her chin. Her eyes were glossy, so I knew she was trying not to cry.

"I know I haven't been a good nigga to you, but one thing I want you to know is that I do love you. I will admit that I never intended on being in a relationship; it was only supposed to be a one-night thing that just so happened to turn into more. Please know and understand that our son was no mistake; he was a gift from God. It's like he was supposed to be born to show me the error of my ways. I won't make excuses for my behavior, and I want to apologize for putting my hands on you and being disrespectful. I just want a clean slate with us… a fresh, new start. Just give me a chance to show you Diamond. I want my family. Outside of my brothers, all I have in this world is you and my son."

"You can't keep hurting me, Judah, and thinking an apology will change things. I hate that you've made me feel like I'm not worthy to be with you. I know that I'm so much more than a stripper who lucked up and got pregnant by a rich ass nigga. It's not about your money, Judah. I love you, I want you, but I don't need you. I'm content with us not being together. All I want is for our son to have both of his parents in his life. I know that you will be a good father to him." She replied, and I ran my hands over my face in frustration. Diamond was talking like it was over between us or something.

"What you saying right now?"

"I'm saying that I need more out of this. You gone have to do more than just say that you love me, Judah St. Pierre. I need you to show me." Diamond stared me down intensely not breaking eye contact.

"What you want me to do, Diamond? You want to get married or some shit. If that's what I have to do to show you that I love you, then I'll do it." I couldn't even believe that I was saying this shit. Judah St. Pierre, a married man. Picture that.

"I would want nothing more but to be your wife. At the same time, I don't want you to do it to shut me up. I want you to do it from the heart, Judah. If it's not from the heart, then it's not real. The shit will crumble. We need to just work on us before we take that leap."

"Well let's start working on that now." I snatched her panties off of her and quickly lifted her up. She wrapped her legs around my waist and kissed me passionately. I roughly pinned her up against the wall. As we continued to kiss I unzipped my pants and let them fall to the floor. Diamond roughly ripped open my button up shirt. I lifted her up just enough so I can slide my dick inside of her.

"Dammmmnn Judah!"

"I'm sorry for everything. Tell me you forgive me."

"Oh shitttt! I forgive you!" I sped up the space as I bounced her up and down on my dick. Just like the pro she is

Diamond was taking all these inches and creaming all over a nigga joint.

"This my pussy Diamond?" I whispered in her ear as I sucked on her earlobe.

"Yasssssss! It's yours Judah." I was nearing my climax and I was ready to release. I didn't give a fuck about her just giving birth to my son. Shit! A nigga was ready to keep her ass knocked up and pregnant because she wasn't going anywhere.

"I love you Diamond and I'm going to get this right."

"You promise."

"I put that shit on everything I love." I stopped bouncing Diamond up and down on my dick so that I could release her. The feeling of her pussy walls clinching my dick let me know she was cumming as well. She wrapped her arms around my neck and held on tight until we were both drained. I slowly walked her over to the bed and laid her down gently.

"I hope you keep your word Judah because I can't keep giving all of me and only getting half of you. Lil Judah and I deserve that much."

"Before I could respond, her phone buzzed, so she reached over and grabbed her phone from the nightstand.

"What's wrong?"

"That's Kenyetta. My brother's girlfriend. She said Kilo at her house tearing shit up. I need to get over there before he has his ass be back in jail. I can't wait to get back home to Dallas." Diamond rushed around the room putting her clothes.

I was ready to get back to Dallas and run the streets with my brothers as well. There was a lot of unfinished business there while I was out in Chicago trying to get my damn girl back. I wouldn't have this conversation with Diamond anymore. I'm just going to have to show her like she wants me to do.

Chapter Eighteen

Kilo

"Please, Kilo don't hit me again!" Kenyetta begged.

I couldn't believe I had to lay hands on Kenyetta. I haven't even been out forty-eight hours, and this bitch had me going across her shit.

"You got my daughter in the next room while you fucking some nigga." I fussed, as I slapped her ass again for being so fucking trifling.

I could hear my daughter crying outside as I placed my key in the door. Granted, I had been away for ten long years, but throughout that time, Kenyetta and I maintained a relationship. I never asked her to wait for me because that would be me being a selfish ass nigga. At the same time, over the years, she'd held a nigga down. Kept money on my books and made sure to visit a nigga every month. One of those visits, we ended up getting married so that we could get conjugal visits, which resulted in her getting pregnant with our now two-year-old daughter.

Kenyetta was more than some bitch that held me down while I was away. She had been my best friend and my wife. She was the reason I made it through them ten years, so walking into the room and seeing her fucking some fat ass nigga drove me over the edge. After I pistol-whooped his ass, I kicked him out, asshole naked.

"I'm sorry, Kilo. Please stop. Kenyarrah is standing here." I looked back, and my daughter was standing in the doorway of the bedroom silent.

She wasn't crying or anything; she was just staring at us. I continued to stand over Kenyetta trying my best not go across her shit again.

"I know that I told you not to wait for me, but damn Kenyetta, you knew I was coming home. What was it? You had to fuck that fat, unattractive ass nigga one more time before your husband came home?"

"No. I had to fuck that motherfucker so you can come home to this." She flipped the mattress over, and it was lined with nothing but rubber bands full of money.

"So wait a minute, you've been fucking him for money." I balled my fist up and walked towards her ass.

"Not necessarily. He was a sweet ass lick. One day I met him, and the nigga was flashing all types of money. He needed to take a trip out to Dallas to see his connect. When we made it up that way, I found his connect was a bitch named Aunt Dot. She runs brothels or some shit out there. From what I gathered, she's hiring a street team to take out some nigga's called the St. Pierre Boys. They're supposed to be some ruthless ass niggas whose mother taught them the game. Big Fred was an easy ass mark, because he took me to his stash house. I've been stealing money from his safe for the last month strictly because I knew I could and he would never find out. That bitch has been giving him so much bread to assemble a group of niggas from Chiraq. He talks too much; I literally know the whole plot. I don't know who them St. Pierre Boyz, but whoever they are, they must be powerful as fuck. They at them nigga's heads.

"I listened to Kenyetta trying to put two and two together. I had heard that name St. Pierre before, but I couldn't put my finger on where.

"Kilo! Kenyetta!" The sound of Diamond's voice brought me back to reality, and it also reminded where the fuck I had heard that name from. It was no coincidence that Judah was from Dallas and that was his last name.

"Pack all that bread up and grab some shit for you and Yarrah; we're about to take a trip to Dallas with Diamond. I'm going to need you tell that same story and everything you know about this damn plot to Judah."

"Who is Judah?"

"Judah St. Pierre is Diamond's nigga."

Chapter Nineteen

Killa Kaam

While sitting at the table in the stash house, I counted out this week's take while puffing a fire ass blunt of Afghan Kush, and that shit had my mind on go. It had been over two days since I last spoke with Don Don, and he didn't tell me shit I wanted to hear. Not only was Maya still missing, but the hoe ass nigga June was playing dumb about her whereabouts. Something inside tells me that he knows more than what he'd been letting on. Don Don put me on about how that nigga went Tony Montana when they popped up at his house. Niggas just don't flip like that for nothing. I got to figure out what's up.

Right when I placed another stack in the money counter, my phone rang, pulling me from my thoughts. Looking down at the screen, I saw that it was my nigga Big Texas. That wasn't really his name, but I gave that to him since he was a huge muthafucka, and he was from Texas.

"Yo, Big Tex, I'm in the middle of something right quick. I'mma have to hit you back." I had stated before he got a chance to start talking.

That nigga was cool as fuck, but he talked a nigga's ear off. Nine times out of ten, he was speaking, and I was listening, but right now, I wasn't in the mood to hear shit unless it was in regards to my fam.

"Nah, my nigga; we need to talk. Don Don nem down here trippin."

Hearing my brother's name made my ears perk up, and I needed to know what the fuck he was up to. He hadn't told me nothing about making any moves.

"What about Don Don?" I quizzed.

"Say, check it; yo bro down here shooting up clubs and shit."

"Okay, and, that's nothing new."

"Fuck that; he not on his turf, and he sparking up a war with some of the most ruthless niggas in Texas; the St. Pierre Boyz. The nigga had a whole shootout with Sebastian St. Pierre, his bitch Dynasty, and other people in the club. I'm surprised they made it out alive. Matter of fact, that's who club they shot up. For me, that ain't even the kicker; they was with that snake ass nigga June. That hoe ass nigga is up to no fucking good and can't be trusted."

I nodded my head in agreeance, because he was telling the truth about June; I had never trusted that bitch ass nigga.

"Yeah, I know he can't but those niggas kidnapped my sister, so it's only right for Don Don to go to war."

"What! You niggas trippin. Last time I heard about some kidnapping shit, it was Maya and June who did the kidnapping. Although the little boy was June's, he was supposed to been dead and his baby momma started fucking with Luxe St. Pierre."

"What the fuck you mean his baby momma. Only Maya got kids with that nigga."

"Nah, you wrong fam; that nigga got a son with this chick Leilani. Her momma used to own a brothel and sold it to them. Her and June turned that shit into one of the hottest strip joints in the city. Word on the street was that when June faked his death, Maya went and took everything from her, including the club, so Leilani burned that shit to the ground."

"Okay, okay, slow the fuck down. You keep saying June faked his death."

"Damn, my nigga; y'all slippin. This some shit y'all supposed to know before y'all go to war." He scolded, and he was right; however, he had better pipe that shit down before his fat ass ended up in a freezer, too.

"I'm gone say this shit only one time. Watch how you handle me, son. You called me to give me some information. Do that, but don't think for one second that I'm gone listen to you say no hot shit while doing it."

He sucked his teeth, "My bad, homie; I'm just saying. Y'all going to war without facts. That's not what's up, but anyway. Yeah, the streets say the nigga faked his death after Luxe St. Pierre shot his bitch ass up."

"And that's the same nigga fucking with his baby momma?"

"Yeah, but I don't think she was on no setup shit, because that hoe loved that nigga's dirty draws."

"Word," I replied in deep thought, because now shit was starting to make more sense.

"Word, and with all due respect, I know you might not want to hear this shit, but yo sister was a grimy muthafucka, too. She wasn't on no up and up. She and June were always fucking over somebody."

"Look, I'm gone hit you back. I got a few calls to make."

"Aight, nigga, I was just calling to put you up on game."

"Respect, nigga," I replied.

"Respect," he said and then hung up.

Standing from the table, I angrily trotted over to the cabinet to retrieve my Remy before I made my call to Don Don. Shit was a lot deeper than the surface, and I needed to get down to the nitty-gritty before things got too far out of hand. After pouring me a glass, I thought on it for a few moments more and decided not to call Don Don. Instead, I shot his ass a text telling him to stand down and then booked myself a flight to Texas; shit was about to get real.

Chapter Twenty

June

Ever since Don Don made it into town, that nigga been watching my every move. I couldn't eat, sleep, shit, or do nothing else in peace. For the past few days, Aunt Dot has been calling my phone, and I needed to step away so we could talk. If not, that bitch was gone be popping up at my doorstep, and she was going to blow my cover for sure. Easing my way into the restroom, I locked the door behind me and cut on the shower to get some privacy and hit Aunt Dot's line.

She answered on the first ring, "About time you answered the damn phone. I thought I was gone have to come by there."

"What the fuck do you want? Ava St. Pierre is dead, so there's no need for you to be hitting my phone no damn mo."

"You better calm the fuck down with that attitude! Don't think I don't know those niggas that you was with."

Hearing that shit made me hush, because I was puzzled to find out what she thought she knew.

"Nah, don't get quiet now big shot. Like I said, I know those niggas is Maya's brothers. Ava put me up on game about them a long time ago. From the looks of things, I gathered that you told them the St. Pierre Boyz was the reason Maya was dead. What other reason would they have to shoot up the club?"

"What the fuck do you want?" I asked, not even replying to her accusation, which was true.

"Look, if you want to get at a muthafucka, you must first kill the head, and the body will fall."

"What the fuck are you talking about?"

She laughed in my ear, "You are as dumb as you fucking look. Wasn't Dynasty the one who popped shit off first at the club? Wasn't she the one who caused the most hell in you and Leilani's relationship? Didn't she go to war with you the night y'all kidnapped Leilani?"

"Yeah, and? You giving her too much credit. Leilani is the brains of everything."

"But she's not the heart; Dynasty is. What you fail to realize is that, that bitch is too smart for her own good, and she peeped everything. Had she not been watching, y'all would've had the drop on Sebastian. Right now, the girl's have those niggas heads so far up their asses that they can't see straight, but Dynasty can. If you listen to me, I can help you break her, which will make it easier for you to get at her and that will also throw the boys off some more. They won't know who the fuck is after them."

"So what's in it for you. Leilani is yo damn daughter; why do you want to hurt her so bad?"

152

"What's in it for me is my business, and why, is my business as well. You just do what the fuck I say, and I'll keep your secret. So, what you gonna do?"

Against my better judgment, I conceded, "Just tell me what you need me to do."

****

At approximately four a.m., my house was completely quiet. After checking around to make sure everyone was sleep, I locked the door to my room and slipped out the window undetected. Pulling my keys from my pocket, I unlocked the door to my bucket and let myself in and headed towards my destination.

To make sure that no one was outside, I circled the block a few times and then pulled into the alley a few houses down. I placed my gloves over my hand, pulled my skully over my face, and screwed the silencer on my gun. Stepping out, I said a quick prayer asking God to forgive me for what I was about to do. There were two people in this world that I had vowed to never fuck with, and that was old people and kids; however, I let Aunt Dot talk me into doing something I was totally against.

Easing into the back gate, I sprinted across the yard and headed for the back door. Knowing that old people were forgetful, I checked under the mat on the porch to see if it was a spare key. After not finding one there, I eagerly searched the entire porch until I came upon a flower pot. Digging my hand inside, I lucked up on something and pulled it out. *Bingo*! I knew she had a key somewhere. Quietly, I stuck the key in the lock and let myself in.

With my gun held high, I tiptoed my way across the kitchen, towards the living room, and then down the hallway. After checking the two rooms along the way, I saw that no one was there, so I kept moving towards the last place at the end of the hall where I heard a TV blasting, so I figured she was probably in there watching one of her shows.

Slowly, I turned the knob and crept the door open to find an elderly lady lying on her back, mouth gaped open, snoring loudly. Not wanting to wake her, I nervously tiptoed across the room and snatched a pillow up from the bed on the side of her. Afterward, I walked around to the other side, placed the pillow over her head, and she began to stir. Wanting to get things done as quickly as possible, I put the gun on the pillow and pulled the trigger three times, killing her instantly. Once I was done, I removed the pillow from her face, threw it on the side, and then prayed for her soul. Damn… that shit had fucked me up.

Chapter Twenty-One

Sebastian

Dynasty's actions had me so pissed off that I didn't even go home last night nor did I call to let her know that I wasn't coming. It was as if the talk I had with her at the club went in one ear and out the other. Not only did she start bussin her guns in the middle of the club, but she also backdoored the next day and got in Luxe and Leilani's business. I don't know why the fuck she was such a livewire, but Dynasty was gone make me 'Judah' her ass, and I don't hit women.

After checking out of the hotel, I sparked a blunt and headed towards the house so we could have one last, much-needed conversation. If she didn't get her act right, I was gone leave her alone. One thing I know is my bitch was supposed to bring out the best in me, not the stress in me, and I was beyond stressed.

"So where the fuck you been all night," Dynasty calmly asked, a little too smoothly for my liking, but I wasn't worried about shit and further opened the door.

Today was the day that I was gone put her ass in check once and for all. She was looking good as fuck, too, wearing one of my button-down shirts, which exposed her toned legs. Her now purple hair was placed in a messy bun at the top of her head, and she wore no makeup, showing off her natural beauty. Still, I ignored her and walked past my living room towards the bedroom with her right on my heels.

"I know you hear me talking to you," she pushed me in the back of my head, and I spazzed.

Before she knew what happened, I swung my body around and wrapped my hands around her neck, picking her up from the floor, "If you knew what was best for you, you would keep your muthafucking hands to yourself. I'm tired of your shit, Dynasty, and I'm not gone give you the chance to bust my lip and shit again."

Her face turned red, and she clawed at my hands mercifully; however, she never asked to be let go of. If I didn't know any better, I think she likes when a nigga gets physical and shit, but that wasn't me, so I dropped her ass. She was turning me into somebody I never wanted to be… my dad. I remember hearing him beat the hell out of Ava and feeling helpless. Although she appeared to be strong all of the time, I knew some things broke her down. Had she been able to live a peaceful life of happiness, maybe she wouldn't have turned out to be the cold-hearted bitch she was, and I'm not going to be the one to turn Dynasty. She was already hell enough.

Seeing her hold onto her neck while trying to catch her breath made a nigga feel real bad, so I scooped her up and carried her to the room. After gently placing her on the bed, I took a seat beside her and looked her straight in the eyes. She didn't say a word, but I could tell by the tears that ran down her face that she was hurt by my actions. Although she is crazy as fuck, I love her with everything in me and never wanted to hurt her more than I already had. That thing with Jazzy, and now this, was more than enough, and I needed her to see that. Using my finger, I tried to wipe away her tears, but she jerked away.

"Look, I know you pissed the fuck off, but I need you to understand that you can't keep putting your hands on me. I don't want you to think that I'm cool with that shit for one second. The only reason why I didn't flip on you that day in the car is because I've never hit a woman before, and I knew I deserved that shit for putting you through the shit with Jazzy."

She turned to face me with a mug on her face, "Okay, I want you to hear me too. The next time you fucking choke me like that it's gone be a muthafucking war. It's gone go either one of two ways; you gone either kill me, or I'm gone kill you!"

"See that right there is the shit I been talking about, Dynasty! Do you fucking think you a man or something? I've bodied niggas for much less, and here you are threatening my life like I'm scared of you. Let's make one thing clear right fucking now; if it ever came down to some shit like that, I would body you without a doubt."

She had me pissed, and I didn't mean to say that, but my mouth kept moving against my brains better judgment.

157

Dynasty hopped from the bed, "Well, let's get this shit popping if that's what you want to do."

I stood from the bed as well, staring her in the eyes, "That's the thing; all a nigga want to do is love on you, but you making that shit hard to do. I don't know what the fuck you've been through, but whatever it is got you fucked up in the head. The only time you are soft is when my dick is inside you. How you gone nurture our future kids with a mentality like that? If you want us to work, you got to let me in, Dynasty. Let me know you, and let me help you get to a softer place in your heart. I'm your man, and you're my woman; we need to act as such."

I pulled her to me, and she tried to snatch away, but I held onto her tightly, wanting her to feel how fast my heart was beating for her.

"Let me go, Sebastian," she whimpered.

"No, Dynasty. I can't, I need you to let me in so I can help you."

She shook her head no, and then laid her head on my chest, crying her eyes out. Right then, I knew it wasn't the time to keep pressing her; she needed to let go of the demons that were eating away at her, and if my arms were where she needed to do it, then I had her. However, this conversation was far from over, and I wasn't gonna stop asking until she gave me an answer.

I turned her to face me and then lifted her off her feet. At the same time, she cupped my face in her hands and began to kiss me passionately while wrapping her legs around my waist. I used my tongue to spread her lips apart and sucked on it lovingly. Without separating our bodies, I gently eased both of us down on the bed and began to place soft kisses on her neck.

Easing up, I looked her directly in the eyes, "I need you to let me in, baby. Let me help you."

Instead of replying, she pulled me closer to her and kissed me again. However, since she thought she was going to shush me, I was going to make her scream into submission. Unbuckling my belt, I kicked off my pants and then rammed my dick inside her. Not expecting me to do that, her eyes widened, and she lifted her body with a deep arch in her back. Cuffing my hands under her cheeks, I thrust myself into her while gazing into her eyes. Nothing more needed to be said; from the look on her face, I could tell that she was feeling my wrath.

"Take it easy, Sebastian, please," she begged, but it fell on death ears.

Flipping her over onto her stomach, I smacked her ass as hard as I could and then entered her from the back. I was pounding every piece of stress she added to my life away on her ass; she needed this. This bitch had me testing my manhood, so I was going to show her one way or the other who was the boss.

Screaming, she looked over her shoulder, eyes pleading with me, as warm liquid gushed from her center. No longer able to hold herself up, she tried to flop down, but I held her ass right there.

"Where the fuck you think you going? You threaten to hurt me, and I'm bout to beat this pussy up. Take that shit like the soldier you are."

"I can't Sebastian," she moaned.

"Are you gone let me in?"

Silence, she just buried her head in the pillow, and I buried my dick further inside her until she couldn't take anymore. Like I said, she had me fucked up, and this pussy was about to get the spanking she needed.

****

After fucking Dynasty for over an hour, she opened up a little more, but my curiosity was getting the best of me. The only thing she told me was that she never felt wanted by any other person besides her grandmother and her brother, so she didn't know how to accept love. She said she knew she loved me from the moment I first spoke to her, but I made her unsure if I felt the same way. Feeling like shit, I kept replaying our conversation over and over again in my head, but I still needed more. Honestly, I believe everything Dynasty told me, but I think she only told me only enough to keep from digging further. If I wanted to know more about her, it was time to meet her grandmother. I know she would keep it real and give me the insight I need to help my baby get right in the head.

Since she was sleeping, I tiptoed to the shower, got dressed, and left out before she woke up from her nap. Jumping in my 2016 Range Rover, I crank J. Cole's album up loudly and lit a blunt before pulling out my yard. Thirty minutes later, I parked in the open parking space at the back of Dynasty's grandmother's home and exited the car with the basket full of wines and cheeses I bought for her along the way.

Nervously, I stood at the door and prayed that she would be as cool as Dynasty said she was. After gathering myself, I knocked on the door, but it opened, and that in itself sent warning bells off.

"Who the fuck is you and why the fuck you at my door," A voice sounded behind me.

Turning around, I noticed a young boy, no older than maybe seventeen; I wasn't sure, but he was mugging me hard as hell.

"I'm Dynasty's man, Sebastian, and I'm here to see your grandmother, Mrs. Lola."

He stepped on the porch, "Okay, I'm Keenan, but why the door open?"

"Shit, yo guess as good as mine, but I know you just saw me knock. I peeped you in the alley when I pulled up. Here," I handed him the basket. "You hold that, and I'mma go in to make sure everything okay."

"Nigga, fuck that; if you going in, I'm going in, too."
He sat the basket on the porch and removed a nine-millimeter
pistol from his waist.

Seeing that, I couldn't do nothing but respect Keenan's
G, and did the same, "You follow behind me. If you see
anything out of the ordinary I want you to shoot first, ask
questions later."

Keenan nodded his head in understanding, and I slowly
entered through the back door.

Whispering over my shoulder, I asked, "Where your
granny's room?" Keenan didn't say a word, he just pointed in
the direction. "Okay, you go check the other bedrooms, and
I'mma go check in there."

"Aight," he replied and went to do what he was told.

With each step closer to the room, the more an uneasy
feeling came over me, and I knew whatever I found would be
no good. Dynasty already had enough shit going on with her,
but if something was wrong with her grandmother, she was
going to fucking lose it. Slowly, I eased the door open and
entered.

"Fuck, fuck, fuck, fuck," I whispered to myself and
paced the floor forgetting all about Keenan being in the
house.

Hearing me, he rushed inside, "What the fuck going…"

Upon seeing his grandmother, Dynasty's brother fell to
his knees, as tears rolled down his cheeks. His face held hurt,
regret, anger, and a series of other things, but that was all I

could make out. Removing my phone from my hip, I dialed 911, and then gave them the address. However, that was the easy part. The hard part was going to be telling Dynasty that her grandmother had been killed.

Chapter Twenty-Two

Dynasty

After Sebastian left, I nervously sat up in bed, with my back leaning against the headboard, constantly replaying our conversation. He was right; I did need to let him in, but it was hard, because I didn't know how. Ever since my mother left me on my grandmother's doorstep, I've dealt with abandonment issues, and the only people I've ever allowed to get close enough to me to know what I was battling internally was my grandmother, my brother, Leilani, and Diamond. When it came to men, I blamed my father for selfishly being such an impact on my mother's life that she chose him over me. Who the fuck does that to their child and continues to live life like she doesn't have kids who need her? I know I should be blaming both parties, but I blame my father more, because he could've made her be the mother that we needed. However, he didn't even try to push the issue.

I was six years old when I learned that Grandma Lola wasn't my mother, and I was crushed, but I quickly got over it. Knowing that I was hurt, she kept apologizing over the years for keeping that from me, but I wasn't mad at her one bit. Hell, she raised me, she gave me love, and she took out the time to nurture me, so technically, she's the only mother I had and would ever have. The day that I met my donor, Fendi, was the day that she dropped my brother off. I remember standing in the doorway staring at her; she was the most beautiful woman on the outside, but she treated me so cold. She never once acknowledged me nor did she even look my way; how pathetic.

Hearing my phone rang, I quickly snapped out of my thoughts and reached to the dresser to grab it. Seeing Sebastian's number made me smile, but at the same time, it made me jittery as hell.

"Hello," I answered, sweetly, like what he would want me to do.

"Bae, I need you to get over here to your grandmother's house. Something has happened, and you need to be here for your brother."

My heart raced to the beat of a pulsating drum as I tried to listen intently to what he was saying, but the only thing I could make out was that something had happened.

"What you mean something happened?" I asked, voice shaken with fear. "Is my brother okay? My grandmother? What is it you not telling me Sebastian?"

"Look, just hurry up and get here. I will fill you in on the rest then."

"No!" I screamed, tell me now.

"Dynasty!" he said my name with authority. "Just do what the fuck I said. Hurry up and get dressed and get here." He replied, and then hung up in my face.

Seeing that I was going to get nowhere with him, I jumped out the bed and grabbed the first thing that I saw to put on. I didn't give a fuck about my appearance, either; I had on a pair of burgundy Addidas sweats, a green BeBe shirt, and a pair of gold slides, looking a hot fucking mess. Grabbing my phone and keys from the dresser, I made a mad dash for the door and jumped in my ride.

Fifteen minutes later, I turned onto my Grandma Lola's street and saw nothing but red, white, and blue lights, surrounding the entire area, and that made my heart drop to my feet. With nowhere else to park, I opted for a space a block away and made a run for the house. Tears dropped from my eyes, my chest felt like it was being squeezed, and my hands sweat profusely. I was a nervous fucking wreck. Dashing past the officers, I ran upon the porch and tried to enter, but I was tackled from the side.

Not giving a fuck that it was the police, I threw a hard blow to his jaw, and he loosened his grip on me.

"Ma'am, you can't go in there. It's a crime scene," an officer stated, and I ignored his ass and kept on going.

"I'm going in there. I don't give a fuck what y'all say. This my muthafucking momma's house."

Sebastian stepped to the door and whispered in the officer's ear.

"I apologize, Mrs. St. Pierre. Come on in. I didn't know you were the victim's family member." The officer apologized, and I fell to my knees.

Looking up at Sebastian and the officer, tears rolled down my cheeks, "What do you mean victim? Did something happen to my grandmother?"

I don't know what made me ask if it was her, but I could feel it deep down in my bones.

Sebastian lifted me to my feet and held me tight, "Yes, baby. Somebody shot her."

"Noooooo!" I screamed and tried to jerk away from him, but he held onto me tighter and wouldn't let me go.

For minutes, we stood right there, and I released all of my troubles on his shoulder, in the comfort of the man who loves me arms. Hearing him sniff, I looked up into his face, and I could tell he was hurting for me just as much as I was hurting for myself. Realizing I had to be strong for Keenan, I finally pushed away and frantically searched the yard for his face.

"Where is my brother? Do he know? Is he okay? Lord, I got to find him. I got to protect him." I started chanting.

"Calm down, Dynasty; he's inside talking to the police. Come on," Sebastian grabbed my hand and led the way inside.

On the sofa with his head in his hands, Keenan sat quietly, seeming to be out of it. Taking a seat beside him, I wrapped my arms around him and leaned my head on his shoulder.

"It's gone be okay, bro; I'm going to take care of us."

He snatched away, "Fuck that! I don't need to be taken care of; I need to get at the muthafuckas that hurt my heart."

168

He punched the wall near him, "Those muthafuckas shot her in the head man; they killed her."

He fell to his knees and cried harder than I had ever seen him cry before. Rushing over to him, I wrapped my arms around him once again, and this time he didn't push away from me. Instead, he wrapped his arms back around me, and we rocked back and forth, comforting each other.

"Come on y'all. The coroner's about to bring her down. Let's walk out for a minute. Y'all don't need to see that right now."

Snapping my head in Sebastian's direction, my eyes held fury, "I need to see her."

"No, Dynasty; you don't need to see her like that. She wouldn't want you to, and you know it."

Releasing my brother, I stood and walked over to Sebastian, staring him in the eyes, "I need to see my grandmother, and I want to see her now. If not, I'm about to set it off in this bitch, and I don't give a fuck about the consequences."

Sebastian shook his head, talked to one of the officer's, whom I presumed was on his payroll, and they signaled for me to follow them

"I'll be right back, Keenan," I informed him before walking way.

Following closely behind Sebastian, we entered her room, and she was lying on a gurney wrapped in a black body bag.

"Are you sure you want to do this?" Sebastian asked, sympathetically, and I nodded my head.

Taking his hand into mine, I shook uncontrollably and held my breath. Moments later, the coroner slowly unzipped the body bag and opened it. Hearing that my grandmother was one thing, but seeing it made me lose my fucking mind. Muthafuckas got to die!

Chapter Twenty-Three

Leilani

There was so much shit going on that I couldn't even focus. The club had been closed down due to the shooting, and some ruthless motherfucker had killed Grandma Lola. Who would do such a thing to her? That was, by far, the sweetest old woman I knew. She couldn't hurt a fly even if she wanted to. Whoever did the shit was heartless and simply didn't give a fuck. To shoot that woman in the head and face like that was overkill. The shit was personal, which leads me to believe this is some retaliation for the shit that's been popping off with all of us.

At first I was thinking someone was after Keenan, but I quickly changed my mind about that. Keenan was a petty hustler, and all his friends were lames. I'm just glad he wasn't in there when they killed her. He would have without a doubt got it, too.

Dynasty had been in such a state of shock that she had literally shut down. Sebastian was going crazy trying to get her out of her funk but nothing was helping. I hated that I wasn't in my right state of mind so that I could be of more assistance. However, I was depressed and taking medication to sleep. I literally can't function. I was having nightmares about June hurting me and Ju-Ju again. Not to mention, I was all in my feelings about this shit with Luxe. I was seeing him and that bitch fucking in my dreams. Luxe hurt me bad with this shit here.

What hurts the most is the fact that he felt like he didn't need to fight for me? His attitude was 'fuck it, and that was the wrong attitude to have. I guess somewhere in my mind I felt like he loved me enough to make it work or try to fix shit, but obviously, he doesn't. If he did, he never would have just dropped me and Ju-Ju off at my house without so much as a goodbye. Granted, I made the decision to leave his home and go back to my own house, but I was in my feelings, and I had every right to be. As bad as I wanted to call him and tell him to come get us, I knew that I couldn't. Just like Luxe has pride, so do I.

******

"I just don't know what to do. I'm so used to her cursing and fighting me. She just sits quietly staring at the wall. How in the hell am I supposed to make her feel better about this?" Sebastian spoke, solemnly, and I felt so sorry for him, because he was really trying his best to cheer Dynasty up.

"All you can do is continue being there for her. Lola was all Dynasty and Keenan has ever had, so this is hard for her. Just you being there and holding her is more than enough. Trust me, she needs that. Sebastian, I've known Dynasty for many years now. Since she's been with you, she has slowed down tremendously. You make her better. Trust me, I know it's hard dealing with her, but she needs you to tell her that everything is going to be okay. All she has is you and Keenan. Just let her ride it out.

If you want me to, I'll come over and stay the night with her. I know you need to get out and put your ear to the streets. I'm not doing shit but sitting in the house depressed over your stupid ass brother anyway. It will do me and Ju-Ju some good to get some air."

"Thanks, Sis. I appreciate it. You and nephew can come over whenever. Just so you know, I appreciate you for stepping in and changing shit for the better. Our businesses have flourished since you came and took over. Not to mention, Luxe has changed. This is the happiest I've seen my Big Bro. That nigga loves you and Ju-Ju. I need to keep it one hundred with you, though. It hurt him for you to question his motives with that June shit. I can't get all into y'all shit, because that would be breaking the Bro code, but just know that he's just as fucked up about it as you are. Love you, Sis. Let me get out of here and get back home to Dynasty. I'll be glad when all of this shit is over. I'm ready to get back to this motherfucking money."

Sebastian and I hugged one another before he left out of the door. I turned around, and Ju-Ju was coming downstairs with his overnight bag.

"Where in the hell you think you're going?"

"My daddy about to come and get me." I pinched the bridge of my nose to calm down. Lately, Ju-Ju had been real flip-mouthed and defiant. I had been holding back because of all that he had been through. Right now wasn't a good time to test me, because I might just beat his little ass. It seems like, ever since we left Luxe' house, he's been in his feelings and getting smart with me.

"I'm not in the mood for your shit today. Go put that bag up. You're not going anywhere." I yelled.

"Yes I am. My Daddy Luxe told me to get dressed. He's on the way for me to stay with him for the weekend." Ju-Ju was looking so happy as he ran past me and towards the door.

The sound of a horn blowing made me rush over to the door as he ran outside. I watched as Luxe pulled into my driveway, and Ju-Ju hopped inside. He cut the music up sky high and quickly backed back out. He didn't even speak or make eye contact with me. My own damn son didn't even say goodbye. My feelings were hurt. Were all the men in my life trying to get away from me? Then again, I knew I shouldn't feel that way. Luxe loves him, and he loves Luxe. Fuck everything else. I'm just glad he's not being punished behind the shit we're going through.

******

"Thank you guys so much for helping me with the service." Dynasty said, as she turned the burners on to keep the food warm. It had been a week since her grandmother had been murdered. Dynasty didn't want her to have a funeral service. Instead, she had her cremated and had a private memorial service, which consisted of only us. She didn't trust a soul after this so she was moving cautiously. We had just made it back from the service and was getting ready to eat dinner at her and Sebastian's.

"No problem. That's what friends are for. I swear you guys have helped me through this thing with Judah." Diamond added.

"I agree. We all we got bitches." I said, as I walked over to them and hugged them both.

We've all been going through some shit lately. It felt good as hell to have Diamond and Dynasty to talk to. Lord knows I didn't have a mother who I could get any advice from. Speaking of her, she'd been trying her best to find out my address. Talking about she wants to come see me and Ju-Ju, but I don't trust her ass as far as I could throw her. After learning that bitch basically gave my club to June, the way I'm feeling I can't even trust myself around her. She has pushed me to a point where I feel like I want to beat her ass and that's my mother so that's not good at all. Dot had been running around with Ava, and anybody who had any dealings with that evil bitch was evil as well. I'm good on that bitch. She could just move on with her life because she will never be in mine.

"So Diamond. Why you didn't tell us your brother was so motherfucking fine?" I sang flirtatiously.

I swear Kilo was sexy as fuck and them dreads didn't make it any better. He was buff as hell. Nigga looked like he bench pressed buildings around this motherfucker.

"Honestly, my life back in Chicago was something I didn't care to bring with me to Dallas. I do apologize for not telling you guys, because we tell each other everything. Kilo may be cute, but he's crazy than a motherfucker. I'm so happy my brother is home I don't know what to do."

"Get this greedy ass baby! He done threw up all over me." Kilo said, as he walked into the kitchen holding JJ.

He was rocking an all-black, linen suit and Ferragamo loafers. Shit, up until now, I thought that Luxe was the only one who made Salvatore Ferragamo look good.

"That's because y'all be shaking him up too much after he eats. Come on, JJ." Diamond grabbed the baby from Kilo, and they both headed out of the kitchen.

"Bitch, you better not let Luxe catch you looking at that nigga for too long. Shit will get uglier than it already is." Dynasty's talking to me brought me out of my trance.

"Girl, ain't shit wrong with looking."

"Unless you want to get fucked up afterwards. What the fuck taking you so long to fix our plates?" Luxe appeared out of nowhere.

"I-I was fixing them now." I stuttered. He walked back out of the kitchen without responding.

"Ahhhh! Bitch, I told you." Dynasty was dying laughing, but I didn't see shit funny. I hurried up and fixed Luxe and JuJu's plate.

That nigga looked like he wanted to kill me. I knew I wasn't that damn obvious looking at Kilo.

"Girl, please. I'm not thinking about Luxe's ass. I hope he did see me looking at Kilo. Serve his ass right for fucking that bitch."

After fixing their plates, I headed into the dining area, but Luxe wasn't in there. I sat Ju-Ju's plate in front of him and went to find Luxe. I looked all around and found him out on the patio talking on the phone. As soon as I stepped outside, he hurried up and hung up his phone. I immediately became angry. I know he was on the phone with that bitch. I felt it in my soul.

"You could have waited until I came back inside to bring me my plate. Why the fuck would you bring my shit out here? You might as well throw that shit away and make me another plate, Leilani. I'm not eating that shit and it touched this dirty, polluted ass air."

"Fuck you, Luxe! I'm not making you shit." I threw the plate on the floor and rushed back inside of the house.

"Leilani! Bring your ass here!"

"What's going on?" Dynasty asked, as she rushed towards me.

"Come on, Ju-Ju. Let's go!" I yanked him up from the chair, but he slipped out of my hand and fell.

"Owwww!" He cried. I went to pick him up but Luxe swooped in and grabbed me by my throat.

"What the fuck is wrong you? I will fuck you up in here, Leilani?" I was clawing at his hands trying to get him to let me go.

This nigga's eyes had turned black, and he was looking like a totally different person. He had me lifted off of the floor in the air.

"Bro, chill?" Sebastian said, as he and Judah tried to remove his hands from around my neck.

"Stop, Daddy! You're hurting her!" The sound of Ju-Ju's voice must have broken him out his trance.

It was as if he realized what he was doing and let me go. I was in a state of shock. I couldn't even cry. I looked around, and everybody was just staring at me, and I immediately became embarrassed. I rushed out of the house and hopped in my car.

"Leilani, wait!" Diamond yelled, but I kept going not trying to hear shit.

I knew that my son was in good hands. I just needed to get far away from Luxe and everybody else for a moment to calm my nerves. Tears clouded my vision as I drove, and my phone was ringing off the hook, but I wasn't answering for anyone up until Ju-Ju's special ringtone blasted. I reached over in the passenger seat for my phone, because I wasn't bout to ignore my baby, but I hit a speed bump and it dropped to the floor, so I bent down to pick it up. When I sat back upright, things happened in a flash, and I didn't have time to shield myself. A car had sped up on the side of me, and a masked man pointed a gun directly at me. With my heart racing, I pressed down on the gas, and tried my best to speed up, but it was too late because the gunman started dumping rounds into my car. I lost control of the car the moment I felt a burning sensation in my chest.

Chapter Twenty-Four

Luxe

The last thing I wanted to do was put my hands on Leilani. I was angry at all the shit that was going on, and I took it out on her. That, added to the fact that I peeped her looking at the nigga Kilo. That shit brought out a new level of craziness inside of me. Her coming out on the patio accusing me of talking to some bitch made me madder. I wasn't thinking about no other bitch. I've been too busy trying to get down to the bottom of this June situation. I was actually on the phone with a nigga who just so happens to know the niggas that shot up the club. Apparently, these motherfuckers are under the impression that we have something to do with the disappearance of their sister Maya. I would bet my last dollar the bitch nigga June planted that seed. It's cool, though, because I'm about to get down to the bottom of all this bullshit. This shit has gone on long enough.

"You wrong for that shit, bruh." I looked at this nigga Judah like he was crazy.

I swear if I had my gun on me I would have given his ass a leg shot. This nigga had big ass balls to address the way I handled Leilani.

"Get your bitch ass out of here, Judah! Just a month ago, you was beating the fuck out of Diamond. Please don't worry about how the fuck I handle my bitch." I had walked up close in this nigga's face and dared him to say some shit, because I was gone clear his ass.

"Nigga, you better back the fuck up out my face." Judah stepped even closer to me. We were damn near nose to nose.

"Both of y'all shut the fuck up and sit down." Sebastian said, as he got in between us.

"Mind your fucking business, nigga. Your bitch beats your ass so you don't have anything to do with this shit here." I pushed his big ass out my face. I was about sick of him and Judah with the bullshit.

"I don't beat his ass; I just don't allow him to do what the fuck he wants to do to me. You just mad because I'm not Leilani, and he can't do or say what the fuck he wants to me. Matter of fact, you better be glad you did that shit to her and not me, because if I was her, I would stab your ass the fuck up. The fuck wrong with you? You just damn near choked the life out of her; she didn't deserve that shit and you know it nigga. My friend is going through it; hell, all of us are going through it fucking with you damn St. Pierre niggas." Dynasty gritted.

"Fuck you just say! That's your motherfucking problem. See, that's what's wrong with you right there; you don't know your place. When you see us men conducting business, you as my woman are supposed to fall back unless I ask you otherwise, but you act like you don't understand shit I'm saying though. You're too busy walking around here acting like a nigga instead of a fucking lady. It's cool, though; I'm officially fed up with your motherfucking mouth. It's some major shit going on out here in these streets, and I don't have time to be dealing with your bullshit." Sebastian said, with an icy glare in his eyes.

"Far as I'm concerned, if you tired of going through shit, then get the fuck on." Dynasty replied.

"You sho muthafucking right. I'll do that, because what you fail to realize is I'm gone be a motherfucking St. Pierre boy until they put me in the dirt, and I'm not gone keep tryna train a bitch to be a lady when she should already know how!" Sebastian replied, fists balled, looking as if he was ready to fight.

For the first time since I met Dynasty, I saw her speechless and not trying to fight. Instead she walked off to the back of the house with Diamond following behind her. I was pissed the fuck off all of this shit was going on in front of Diamond's brother and his girl. Quiet as it was kept I was mad at Judah and Diamond for even bringing them here. They know we keep our motherfucking circle small, and I don't want perfect fucking strangers sitting around me and my family.

"Can we please sit the fuck down and talk about moving on these fuck niggas? Bro, I need you to hear this shit Kilo girl knows. This shit is going to blow your mind." Judah said.

183

He had been telling me about some shit he found out back in Chicago, but I hadn't had time to get with him. I wanted to kill this nigga Kilo. Parading around my bitch with them damn dreads, showboating. I peeped her looking at that nigga. She lucky I didn't blind her motherfucker ass for the blatant disrespect.

"Yeah, let's talk about that. I need to get the fuck out of here and go find Leilani. I looked over and saw Ju-Ju staring at me looking sad. Instead of following my brothers to Sebastian's office, I went over to talk to him. I felt like shit because I was the reason he was looking sad.

"Is my momma coming back?"

"Yeah, she's coming back. I made her mad, so she had to go and get some air. I'm sorry that you had to see me do that. I was wrong. A man should never treat a lady like that. I love you and your momma very much. After I go and talk to your uncles, I'm going to go get her and bring her back. Okay?" Ju-Ju wrapped his arms around my neck and hugged me tightly.

Lil Nigga made me tear up a little. Ever since I met him and Leilani they've etched away all the ice around my heart. Just looking at him upset about her leaving let me know that I needed to hurry up and go find my baby. In my heart, I know that I love Leilani. She gives me purpose. Having her in my life shows me that, all that shit Ava was talking was pure bullshit. Love won't do shit but make you a better person than you already are. I know it sounds crazy, but I'll be the first to admit that Leilani has done just that. I'm just a nigga

184

who's stuck in his ways. Before heading back to chop shit up with my brothers, I hugged Ju-Ju once more. I was glad that he had calmed down, but I could tell he really wanted Leilani to come back. I had every intention of going to get her. I just hoped she would forgive me for choking her. As soon as I headed in the direction of Sebastian's office, my phone rang. I answered it, and I immediately lost my cool and start punching the wall and kicking it.

"Fuck! Fuck! Fuck!" I said, as I hit my forehead several times.

"What the fuck, Bro?" Sebastian said, as he surveyed the holes in the wall. I composed myself and said it low so that the girls or Ju-Ju couldn't hear me.

"We need to get up to the hospital. Leilani was in an accident. A nurse just called me and told me I needed to get up there quick. Why the fuck did I spazz on her like that?"

"Calm down. Let's just head up there to the hospital. Leilani a rider, so I know Sis cool." Judah said, as he tried to stop me from hitting something else. I took giant ass steps damn near running getting out of the door trying to get to the hospital. I wanted to think positive, but the nurse that called me sounded sad. *What if she didn't make it?* I thought to myself, as I sped out of the driveway. I looked in the rearview mirror and saw my lil brothers right behind me. No matter what, we're always here for one another.

******

"Excuse me, Sir! Can I help you?" I rushed through the emergency unit with Sebastian, Judah, Dynasty, Kilo, and his girl close behind me. Diamond stayed back with the kids.

"I'm looking for Leilani Brooks; a nurse called me and told me she had been brought here."

"Oh yes! That was me; you were listed as her emergency contact. Please have a seat; I'm going to page the attending. He should be out to talk to you and the family shortly." The nurse quickly walked way from us and went back over to the intake area.

"These motherfuckers need to tell me something about my friend!" Dynasty yelled and went after the nurse. I hoped like hell we didn't get kicked out this motherfucker.

"Let me grab her. Dynasty's ass is banned from this hospital after she bussed June shit with that damn bedpan."

"It's okay. I'll try talking to her. Stay here with your brother." Kilo's girl had gotten up and went after her.

"We got to stop this bullshit! Ava is still wreaking havoc from the grave against us."

"What you mean, Big Bro?" Judah asked me.

"What he means is, all this damn fighting we doing with Leilani, Diamond, and Dynasty is exactly what the fuck she wanted. Shit been all bad for us since she showed her true face. I'm with Luxe. I'm tired of fighting with Dynasty. I love her. Even if she is Bipolar."

"I'm not going to even front. I love Diamond, and I'm ready to settle the fuck down. Ava will not continue to fuck up my frame of mind. I just want to get this bread and take care of my family." I sat listening to my brothers and realized that they weren't little boys anymore. They had grown into men. It was at this moment I knew they didn't need me to tell them how to treat women or what types to fuck with. They had already found the best in everything I tried to steer them away from. I was without a doubt wrong for the way I viewed them when we first met, including Leilani.

"Just take advantage of them being here and safe. I might have lost my chance at loving the only woman I've ever loved." As I finished my statement, I noticed a doctor walking with the nurse that I had talked to earlier. I quickly stood to my feet as they approached us.

"Hello, Mr. St. Pierre. I'm Dr. Shalome. I treated your wife when she came in. She sustained multiple gunshot wounds prior to hitting a tree.

"What the fuck you mean multiple gunshots? You're telling me a motherfucker shot her, and that's how she had the accident."

"Don't quote me on that, but it looks that way. The police were here, but she was taken up to surgery. She was unconscious when they brought her in. During my assessment, and after running test, we learned that she is about eight weeks pregnant. Right now, the fetus is okay. Miraculously, none of the bullets did any damage to it. This is a first with me. All of the trauma her body sustained it's mindboggling that the baby did make it this far. However, the bullet that concerns me is the one that hit her in the chest, which caused her lung to collapse. She made it out of surgery, but right now, we have her in a medically-induced coma. We'll see how she does the next forty-eight hours.

I will tell you that there is a possibility that the fetus might not be able to survive all that Ms. Brooks is going through, but we are trying our best to bring both of them out of this alive. I'll be on call for a couple more hours monitoring her. You can go back and see her shortly."

I sat down in the chair trying to gather my thoughts. I can't believe these motherfuckers shot her like that. Not to mention the fact that she was pregnant. Hearing that revelation made me feel even worse about the fighting that we had been doing. Leilani had to make it out of this. She had to be strong for our seed.

"What the fuck this bitch doing here?" Judah said, breaking me from my thoughts.

I looked up, and it was Dot with two big cocky ass niggas. Her presence had me thinking. How in the fuck did she know Leilani was here? The bitch is not listed as a contact. The streets ain't heard this shit just yet. Dot is going to make me kill her motherfucking ass if I find out she had anything to do with what the fuck happened to my baby. In the meantime, I was about to play right with this bitch to see where her head was at.

"Excuse me; what is going on here; I'm trying to find out what's going on with my daughter Leilani Brooks." Dot stated, dramatically, to the nurse with snot and tears running down her face.

Standing from my seat, I walked in Dot's direction just in time to hear what the nurse had to say.

"I'm sorry, ma'am; the doctor had to rush into another surgery, so it may take some time for him to come out and speak to you. However, I can try to see if I can get one of the other doctors to come out and ease your mind."

"Yeah, you do whatever it is you need to do, because I need to speak to someone now!" Dot slammed her hands on the desk.

"Hold the fuck up!" I interrupted her fit. "What the fuck you doing here, and how you know something happened to Leilani that fast?" I quizzed.

Dot angrily turned to face me with a mug on her face; "It's all your damn fault she's in here, and you have the nerve to walk over here like you big and bad to question me. In case you forgot, I'm her momma, and my daddy is dead, so I don't have to answer shit you ask. Right now, I should be asking you what the fuck you doing here? You not no kin to her; hell, y'all not even married."

Before I knew it, I had grabbed Dot by her neck and slammed her back into the nurses' station. The two big, burly muthafuckas she had with her tried to rush me, but they didn't have a chance because Sebastian and Judah were on their asses. Standing in front of the dudes, they flashed their weapons where only we could see, and the dudes angrily fell back.

With murder in my eyes, I looked down at Dot and spoke through clenched teeth; "If I ever hear you speak Leilani's name, hear about you looking for her, or you step within one-hundred feet of her, I'm gone end yo muthafucking life. See, I was gone try to play nice with yo bitch ass, but I'm not stupid; I know you had something to do with this shit happening to her. The streets don't talk that fast, so you shouldn't have even known she was here. Now check it, I'm gone give you bitches a pass for now, so your best bet is to grab these two pussies with you and leave before I change my mind."

Releasing her neck, she slid to the floor, and I took a step back, waiting for her to make one wrong move. Before attempting to get up, she sucked in massive amounts of air to catch her breath, rolled over onto her knees, and then lifted her body from the floor. Fake tears slid down her face, and she pretended to look at me sorrowfully, but I knew better.

"You're wrong about this, Luxe; I love my daughter, and I will never do nothing to hurt her."

"Bitch, cut the bullshit and get the fuck outta here before I kill yo bitch ass." Judah intervened, and I placed my arm across his chest to get him to stand down; this was not the time nor the place.

Knowing that she was living on borrowed time, Dot ordered her goons to follow her and quickly headed for the exit.

Chapter Twenty-Five

Dynasty

My mind was in a dark place, as I paced back and forth in the parking lot at the hospital. Too many things had happened, and I was starting to feel like I was failing my people. The one's who I was supposed to protect. With tears streaming down my face, all I could think about was how someone took my grandmother's life, and now Leilani was laid up in the hospital, and I was on the brink of losing my sanity.

"Stop, Dy! Are you listening to me?" Kenyetta screamed, so I turned to face her with a murderous look in my eyes.

I hadn't known that bitch long at all, and she had already given me a name. I wasn't tripping, though, because Dy fit me, especially since I was about to start causing a whole bunch of muthafuckas to die.

"Kenyetta, I fuck with you, boo; I really do, but now is not the time. Any moment now, I'm bound to snap, and I don't want it to be on none of y'all, so let me be, please. I just need a few moments to myself to calm down."

She waved me off like she didn't care about shit I said, "Fuck that; I got to put y'all up on game. From the time we got here, I been tryna tell y'all what I know, but y'all got so much shit going that I haven't been able to get it out. I know I don't know y'all well enough to interfere, but I'm telling you that what I know may be linked to what's happening to y'all."

"Aight, go head, and this better not be no bullshit, because we gone fall out for real for real," I warned.

She placed her hand on her hip and chuckled lightly, "Look bitch, I'm not trippin on getting into it with nobody, because I does this gangsta shit, too. I don't know how Leilani and Diamond rock, but I guarantee that me and you, we rock on the same level, so if you respect my G, I'mma respect yours."

Any other time, and with any other bitch, it would've gone down, but I can respect a bitch who is "G" like me, as she says; however, we'll see about that. If and whenever shit gets hot, she better be down to ride, or I'm revoking her card like uh muthafucka.

"You got that; so what's up?"

"Okay, so before Kilo came home, I met this trick ass nigga that talked to much. The nigga was a real easy ass lick, so I was stinging his ass for his cash. Anyways, he took me on a trip with him to Dallas to meet up with his connect named Aunt Dot."

I put my hand up to stop her, "Wait, hold up; did you say, Aunt Dot?"

"Yes, bitch, but when it comes to her, all I know is that she runs or ran a brothel or some shit like that. Listen, though… from what I gathered, she'd been working hard to hire a street team to take out the St. Pierre Boyz. I didn't know who they were until Kilo brought Judah and Diamond over. Girl, that bitch was giving him so much bread to assemble a group of niggas from Chiraq to take them out, but that's over with, because Kilo and Judah shut that shit down while they were there. Before we left, they ended up killing the nigga who set the shit up, but I don't think Aunt Dot is gonna stop."

Hearing that made my heart pump rage. Out of all people, I thought she would have learned her lesson, but nah, this bitch wanted to take it there.

"Man! I'm gone murder that bitch! I don't give a fuck bout her being Leilani's momma!"

"What? That's Leilani's momma?"

"Yes, gi…" I started to say, but Kenyetta pointed and whispered.

"Hold on, Dy; that look like that's her right there."

To make sure I wasn't trippin, I turned my head in the direction she was pointing so fast that I almost snapped my neck, and I'll be a monkey's ass; it was Dot, and she was right on time. I checked my bag to make sure my gun was in there and then started walking to my car without saying a word.

"Hold on, Dy; where you going?" Kenyetta asked, while following close behind.

I stopped dead in my tracks causing her to run into the back of my heels, "You say you G, right. Okay, I'm 'bout to go murder these bitches, so you got two choices. You can ride with me, or you can go back upstairs with the men, but either way, I'm about to handle up."

Kenyetta pulled a strap from her back with a goofy grin on her face, "Let's go. I ain't got into no funky shit in a long time. Oh, and by the way, don't be tryna test my gangsta. I ain't running up the stairs to them niggas."

After Dot and her goons hopped into their vehicle, both Yetta and I trotted towards my car and the chase began.
****

Murder, murder, kill, kill, were words that I unconsciously kept repeating over and over in my head as I inconspicuously trailed Dot's vehicle three car lengths behind. I didn't know exactly what was happening to me, but what I did know was, right then, I felt something inside of me that was even more violent than anything I'd ever felt before. As I bent the corner behind Dot, all I could see was red. Red streets, red clouds, red birds, red trees, red lights; hell, red everything! However, on the outside, I appeared to be cool, but on the inside, I was hyped as hell, because I was about to get to release the havoc that had been bottled up inside. I know it wasn't going to bring my granny back, but it was for damn sure the first step to getting me back in my right mind.

After thirty minutes of driving, they turned onto a one-way street in South Dallas, and that shit was great, because it takes the laws forever to get out here. Niggas could have WWIII on these streets, and they wouldn't have to worry about the police coming to stop them. This area was as ruthless as I was about to be.

As I pulled over a few houses down from where they parked, I looked over at Kenyetta, and she was typing away on her phone. She probably was texting Kilo the address where we were, and he most likely was going to tell Sebastian, but I didn't give a fuck. That nigga wants to say I think I'm a man, then fuck him, too. Don't play with me; I'm all woman, and he knows it, because he can't keep his face out the plate between my legs, ole bitch.

Hearing Kenyatta pull the hammer back on her pistol as she put one in the chamber brought me out of my thoughts, and I nodded my head in approval.

"Alright then, bitch; let me find out you ready to get into this gangsta shit," I said in a joking manner but was serious as hell.

She cocked her head to the side with a grave expression on her face, "I told you I do this; you better ask Kilo about me. Now, is you ready, or you gone sit here watching me some more? Yeah, I saw you, heifer." She smirked, knowingly.

Looking up at the night's sky, I quietly said a quick prayer and repented for what I was about to do. Although inside I'm a killer, I know right from wrong, and I often apologized for the things I'd done. I just hoped God was still listening to me.

Pulling the door handle, I threw over my shoulder, "Let's get it."

Following my lead, Kenyetta hopped out the car behind me, and we tiptoed our way through the neighbor's yard. We crept like a G to the back of their house and looked in, but all the lights were out. I looked around to see if there were any windows I could possibly find open, but they all were barred up, so that was a no-go. Hoping they were slipping, I grabbed the door, but it was locked, so we did the next best thing and kicked that muthafucka off the hinges. One of the guards that were with Dot tried to draw his gun, but he was too slow.

Bock! Bock! Bock!

I let my pistol bark like a dog and popped his bitch ass right between the eyes. Right behind me, Kenyetta swung to the right just in time, catching his friend once in the stomach and one in the dome.

As I stepped over one of the pussies, I punted his head so got damn hard that his neck sounded like it cracked. With her guns raised high, Kenyetta moved passed me and peeped her head around the corner to see if it was anyone else coming towards us. Once she saw the coast was clear, she signaled with her arm for me to follow behind her. While she traveled down the hall facing the front, I was walking backward, and we were back to back, both on a mission to not get caught slipping. Good thing for us, it was only a small two-bedroom home, so we didn't have far to go. While she checked the first bedroom, I checked the restroom, and once we saw that they were clear, we continued on our way to the last room.

No sooner than I grabbed the knob to go in, shots rang out, and we both dove to the side to not get hit. Listening intently, I counted the shots that rang out. I pretty much had an idea of what size clip it was they had, but I couldn't be too sure.

"Fourteen, fifteen, sixteen, seventeen," I counted, barely above a whisper, and when the fire ceased, I sprang from around the corner and kicked the door open to find Dot trying to reload her gun, and Jazzy lying on the floor with her arms covering her head. After seeing Jazzy, I was thrown off my square just a little bit, but not enough to not peep Dot trying to move. Walking past me, Yetta popped Dot in the shoulder with a hot one, and she flew into the wall behind her. With a huge grin on my face, I walked over to Jazzy and kicked her stank ass in the face.

"Get up, bitch! I've been looking all over for you." I sang, while snatching her up from the floor by her hair.

Peeking out the corner of my eye, I saw Yetta standing over Dot with her gun trained on her, and the look on her face was daring Dot to make a move. Right then, I knew I liked that bitch, and we were gone be cool as fuck.

"Bitch, I know you didn't think it was going to be over after you hit me with that got damn tire iron." I spat before clocking Jazzy's ass upside the head with my pistol.

She screamed out in pain and quickly tried to cover her face, but I dove right on top of that ass. Over and over, I brutally smacked her with my gun releasing all of the pent-up frustration I had in me. My granny was dead, Sebastian broke up with me, my brother talking about calling our bullshit momma, Jazzy left me to die in the park, and Leilani being in the hospital was a toxic combination. As I continued to beat her, blood splatters were flying everywhere, and my shirt was soaked. Tired, I lifted her from the floor once again and pushed her against the wall.

"Say your prayers, bitch," I gritted, as I stuck my pistol in her swollen mouth, which was hanging open.

No sooner than my finger grazed the trigger, I felt someone tackle me into the wall behind me, and the gun went off.

"Nooo! Don't kill her yet, Dynasty." Sebastian begged with pleading eyes.

"Get the fuck off me," I screamed, and then I kneed him in the dick making him release me.

"Dammit," he mumbled, as he toppled over in pain.

With tears sliding down my face, all I could do was shake my head, because this nigga saved that bitch yet again after all she had done.

"Damn, Sebastian; so this how we doing it? You gone spare this bitch's life after she tried to kill me. Damn, you love her that much? How can you do me like this when I've had your back? I've killed niggas for you, nurtured you back to health, and loved your child like he was my own, even after Jazzy did that hoe shit."

Sebastian stood up as straight as he could and started hopping in my direction, "No, it's nothing like that, Dy…"

Before he got to finish his sentence, I slowly lifted my arm with my eyes looking directly into his and pulled the tripper.

Pop! Fuck what he was talking about; I shot Jazzy's hoe ass in the shoulder, because there was no way I was letting her walk out of here with only an ass beating. Nonetheless, it didn't make me feel any better, because I didn't get to kill her like I wanted to. Turning on my heels, I briskly walked past Kilo, and Judah while listening to Sebastian repeatedly call my name. However, I didn't stop nor did I turn around; I just kept on going to my car with Yetta jogging behind me.

Yetta's sat in the passenger's seat while looking at me as if she wanted to say something, but she opted to keep quiet because of the situation. However, I hate a bitch to bite their tongue, so I spoke up.

"You look like you want to say something; go ahead. I'm listening."

"Nah, I'm gone just keep my thoughts to myself, because right now, you heated, and I'm not tryna get into it with you."

I sucked my teeth irritably, "Yeah, I'm pissed right now, but not at you; especially after you had my back like you did tonight. Thank you."

"You don't have to thank me, because I know you would've done the same for me if I was emotionally unstable like you are right now."

Highly offended, I glanced in her direction, "Who the fuck you calling emotionally unstable?"

"I'm talking to you, ain't I? You are the only other person in the car that's going crazy right now."

"Bitch, I ain't going crazy. I want revenge."

She nodded her head, "I understand that, trust me I do, but you're not focused enough to be trying to get revenge on nobody. From what I saw back there, you would've probably got hurt if I wasn't with you."

"How can you say that when I busted my guns just like you?"

"You did, but you also paused in the kitchen. We didn't know how many people were in that house, so once you took out one of those niggas you should've been on high alert for the other, and what about when you saw that chick? Yo undivided attention went to her, and if Dot really knew what she was doing, yo ass would've been shot."

"You right, that was my mistake; I just wasn't expecting to see Jazzy there."

"I ain't the smartest cookie in the jar, but I do know I can't let shit distract me when we at war. And I don't even want to talk about Sebastian!"

"Alright now, bitch, tread lightly," I warned, because even though I'm mad, I won't play about him.

"Damn, calm down. I wasn't even about to say nothing about him on the level you thinking, but I do want to say I know what he's talking about with you."

"I hope you ain't tryna that say I'm a man."

Yetta giggled, "Nah, I'm not saying that, but I am saying that you act like you too stubborn to allow Sebastian to be the man, and with that, you're killing his ego. Here's the thing, when it comes to the kind of caliber of men that we have; we got to play our position, and when I say that, I'm not saying it as if we got to jump at their beck and call like their maids. However, we do have to let them think they're running shit. No man wants to look like his bitch is the one who wears the pants, especially in front of other people. For example, when Kilo is talking to the other men, I sit quietly, and only speak when I'm spoken to. I do that for two reasons; one is to stroke his big ego, and two, is so I can get an earful. One thing my momma taught me is that a lady is better to be seen than heard, and her presence speaks volumes for her."

"You right; it's just hard to change how I've been all my life," I whispered. "I'm so scared to give him that much authority, because if he fucks me over, I'm going to kill him."

"Bitch, he's not going to fuck over you. When he looks at you, all I can see is the love he has for you. You are crazy as hell; all that man wants you to do is allow him to love on you, but you making it hard. Whatever it is that got you off your game right now, I need you to pray about it and try to let it go before you lose your man and your life. You went off on him

203

for saving that bitch, but I don't think that's what he's doing. Shit, think about it, Dy; why was she with Dot anyway? They could be plotting to get y'all, and y'all would have no clue if you would've killed them right then. Hell, he was thinking smart."

Everything Yetta said was the truth, and I couldn't even argue. If I wanted to keep the only man that I've ever loved, then I better make some changes and make them quick. I don't know how I'm going to do it, nor how long I will last, but I do want to try, because I love Sebastian just as much as he loves me, and I for damn sure don't want anyone else.

Chapter Twenty-Six

Sebastian

"Shit! Man, I got to go get Dynasty. Call the cleaners to come get this mess up, and y'all take these bitches to the house out in Joppy." I ordered.

"Nigga, I know what to do. You just go do what you got to do to make shit right with my sister. I don't give a fuck how much you want her to be like everybody else; nigga Dynasty is the fucking truth and you'll be a damn fool to let her get away." Judah replied.

I nodded my head, "You right about that shit. Seeing all the damage they done up in here made my dick hard as fuck, so I got to get right with her for real if I want to get the edge off."

"Hold up, nigga; ain't not they." Kilo interrupted, causing me to laugh.

"You right, I was referring to my bitch only, nigga. Stand down killa." I joked. "Now, let me go so I can go empty these nuts."

"TMI nigga, damn; just leave." Judah waved me off.

Remembering the pain I saw etched on Dynasty's face devastated me. Before now, I didn't understand how much my actions had negatively impacted her. If she thought for one minute that I was trying to save Jazzy's life, then she was crazier than I imagined. Fuck that bitch, Jazzy; she got to die for trying to set me and my brothers up. That chump change she stole from me was nothing. I'm more pissed about her abandoning our son, and I can only imagine how Jr is feeling. Although he seemed to be happy, I know he misses her, and it's fucked up that she'd put me in a position to have to kill her.

On 120, I had the pedal pressed to the metal doing one-hundred-five in a sixty trying to get to my baby. She can't leave me, and I'm not leaving her; I love her too much. I know what I said earlier was fucked up, and I regret every word that came out of my mouth. Ever since the day I met Dynasty, she's been solid, and no matter how mouthy she is, I couldn't take that away from her at all.

As I slid the key in the keyhole, I silently prayed that she would hear me out, because I wasn't prepared to let her go. Upon entering, I noticed the house was completely dark, but I could hear whimpering coming from the dining room. Quickly walking in that direction, I turned on the lights to find Dynasty, with her head rested on her arms crying her eyes out. Not knowing where her head was at, I slowly approached her and rubbed my fingers through her hair.

"I'm so sorry, Baby; I never meant to hurt you. It's not what it looked like."

She slowly lifted her head and gazed at me, eyes swollen and nose red. With her sleeve, she wiped her nose and then stood from her seat.

"I'm sorry, too, Sebastian; right now I'm broken and don't know how to be fixed. This is me, this is a part of me, and if you can't be patient enough to teach me how to love, then we can't keep doing this. I don't want you unhappy, but you also can't force me to be somebody I'm not."

Grabbing her into my arms, I pulled her close and held onto her tightly, "Fuck that, I'm not going nowhere, and neither are you. We just got to get some type of understanding. Come on," I grabbed her by the hand and led her towards the bedroom. "Let's lay down and talk."

****

"I hope you got shit together," Judah asked as he took a seat at the table with me and Luxe.

"Yeah, nigga we good. It ain't nothing that St. Pierre dick can't fix." I joked.

For a few moments, me and Judah threw shots back and forth while Luxe sat quietly appearing to be in his own world.

"Fuck all that!" Luxe slammed his hand on the table. "I'mma need you niggas to get serious, because shit ain't been adding up."

"What shit?" I asked.

"I'm talking about all the shit that's been happening. The club being shot up, Grandma Lola getting killed, Leilani being shot, and then this shit with these NY niggas. What the fuck they got to do with anything?"

"Oh yea, what's up with them niggas?" Judah interrupted.

"I don't know, but we got a meeting with them later on tonight. From what I gathered, the niggas at our heads because of the Maya bitch."

"The one that shot Juju? What the fuck those niggas got to do with her. That bitch got what she deserved shit," I replied. "Oh, yeah, and we got Dot and that bitch Jazzy at the spot over in Joppy. Kilo's girl told Dynasty that she was tryna get some niggas from the Chi together to hit us."

"Fuck it, I have a feeling those bitches got something to do with the shit. One of y'all go grab them, and I'm going to set shit up at the club. I don't need no fucking surprises."

"Aight, bet! I'll go grab them." I slapped hands with Luxe and then Judah.

After that, we all went our separate ways; it was time to get down to business.

****

"Load these bitches in the back of the van and follow behind me to the club." I ordered the youngin' I had watching over the girls.

"Bruh, I got you, but one of the bitches looks like she damn near about to die."

"I don't give a fuck if the bitch die on the way. Load the bitches up and let's go."

He raised his hands in the air in surrender, "You got it Boss; I'll have them loaded up in less than five.

While I waited for them to get Dot and Jazzy in the van, I hit Dynasty up to see what she had going, but she didn't answer. After the conversation we had last night, I knew she was feeling a little better, but I still was worried about her. She was a loose cannon. Placing my phone back in my pocket, I jumped in the driver's seat and watched as they pulled Dot out kicking and screaming.

"You fuck ass niggas won't get away with this. I got something for y'all bitch ass." She screamed, while my youngin dragged her by the hair to the truck.

"Shut up, bitch," the youngin slapped her ass and then forced her into the back.

Jazzy, who looked to be out her mind and weak, didn't put up a fight, and I'm glad she didn't because I didn't want to have to fuck her up before we got any of our questions answered.

The youngin' tapped on the back of the van, "We're all set to go."

No sooner than I got ready to pull off, a car came from nowhere and slammed into the front of the van, followed by three Suburbans in front blocking my way. Caught completely off guard, my head banged into the steering wheel and blood poured from a gash over my eye. The youngin and two other of my soldiers saw the commotion and immediately started dumping at the trucks; shoot first, ask questions later. With my blood pumping adrenaline, I eagerly tried to release the buckle, but I was stuck. Thinking quick, I removed the knife I always carried from my back pocket and started cutting through the seatbelt. Meanwhile, around me, it was a war going on, and we were outnumbered. Shots were coming from everywhere, and I was pissed, because I couldn't get out the seatbelt any faster. Cutting through the last piece of fabric, I yanked the belt, and opened the door.

Finally!! I thought to myself while removing my pistol from my hip. I watched as the back door opened to one of the trucks and a muthafucka stepped out with a rocket launcher. One foot was on the ground when I took a dive, but it was too late…Boom!

Chapter Twenty-Seven

Luxe

"Where the fuck is Sebastian?" I asked Judah, as I looked down at my watch for the tenth time.

"I don't know; I talked to him a lil while ago, and he said he was on his way." Judah replied.

"Aight, where's Kilo?"

"He ducked off at the back in case something goes wrong."

The meeting was due to start in five minutes, and Sebastian still hadn't made it with Dot and Jazzy. Knowing Sebastian, his ass was trying to make sure everything ran smoothly or he was either driving like somebody's grandpa to get here, so I wasn't too worried.

"Kilo just hit me and said that he saw the New York niggas walking to the door now." Judah tapped my shoulder.

"That's what's up. Go meet those niggas at the door and bring them to the table."

"What's up? You Luxe?" a dark-skinned dude with a mouth full of gold teeth and dreads asked with a heavy NY accent."

"Yea, that's me." I replied and then took a sip of my drank. "Have a seat."

Behind him stood four other dudes, and they all had their game faces on, but none of that shit fazed me. These niggas were on my territory.

Pulling out a seat, two dudes took a seat, "I'm Killa Kaam, and this is my brother Don Don."

"Look, fuck all that. Let's get down to business, because the last time you were in my club, it was a muthafucking shoot-out, and I don't play that shit. This is my place of business, and it has been disrespected like a muthafucka." I said, cutting straight through the bullshit.

Removing my pistol from my waist, I sat it on the table, but never removed my hand. Following my lead, Don Don quickly stood from his seat and pointed his gun at me, and Judah walked up with his pointed straight at Don Don. After that, the rest of the men followed suit.

Killa Kaam raised his hand for Don Don to chill, "If shooting it out was what we set out to do I can guarantee we wouldn't have called this meeting. I'm just looking for my sister Maya."

"You talking about the same Maya that shot my muthafuckin nephew." Judah spat.

Killa Kaam looked at Judah and then back towards me, "So is that shit true?"

"Do we look like we'd be playing about some shit like this? That fuck ass nigga June, Jazzy, and Maya kidnapped my wife and my son, and while they were there, Maya fucking shot my lil nigga." I replied through clenched teeth.

212

"From what I heard, you niggas kidnapped my sister."
Don Don spoke up.

Judah laughed, "That's what you get for listening to bitch
ass niggas; I know only June told you that shit."

Don Don turned his gun on Judah, "Nigga, you talk too
fucking much. Do it look like we talking to you?"

"When you talk to one St. Pierre Boy you talking to us all
nigga. Fuck you thought this is."

"Don Don, chill nigga!" Killa Kaam demanded.

"Yea, chill nigga; yo brother got your best interest at
heart." Judah taunted.

"Fuck the guns, nigga. We can box it out." Don Don
challenged Judah.

"You ain't said shit but a word, nigga; let's get it." Judah
winked.

"Fuck all that shit! Judah, chill." I instructed him and then
turned to Killa Kaam. "Look, as far as yo sister go, she dead
as a muthafucka, and it ain't nothing bringing her back, but
you after the wrong niggas. If you gone be mad at anybody,
you should be mad at that nigga June. Not only was it my
wife's son she shot, but it was June's. That nigga is just as
much responsible than anybody, and just like you will go to
war for yours, I'll go to war for mine. Yo sister wasn't right."

"Speaking of June, here that bitch ass nigga go right here. I
caught him snooping around back." Kilo interrupted, as he
pushed June into VIP.

June fell forward onto his knees with fear in his eyes.

Killa Kaam turned his attention to June, "Bitch ass, nigga, I knew you had something to do with this shit."

"These niggas lying." June pleaded.

"Oh yeah," I said, as I pulled my phone from my pocket to show Killa Kaam Juju's picture. "There's no need to lie; the lil nigga looks just like his bitch ass." I handed Killa Kaam the phone.

His eyes traveled back and forth from June to the picture, and he shook his head.

"Aight, but who killed Maya?" Killa Kaam turned his gun on me.

Before I got to speak, loud claps could be heard coming from behind me, which caused me to divert my attention in that direction, and in walked about ten niggas.

"Ava told me you boys was pussies. Who the fuck explains anything to another neega. You bwoys are soft. Nothing like me."

"Who the fuck are you and how did you get past my men?" I asked, while willing myself to not pull the trigger just yet.

He snickered, "I would've thought you would be able to see the similarity being that we look the most alike, brother. Oh, and your men… all dead. It was rather easy, too."

"Bitch, you not my brother." Judah jumped in.

"Oh, but contrare, little Judah; we all have the same Ice Queen's blood pumping through our veins. The only difference is she was taken away from me, and she was able to raise you all. I'm your long lost brother; Ava's oldest son."

"Man, ain't this some bullshit! What the fuck you niggas got us in the middle of?" Killa Kaam spat.

"Oh, don't worry. I will be gone in a minute. I just came here to tell my brothers that the St. Pierre Boyz will be stepping down, because the Baptiste Mafia is now in charge."

"Over my dead body." I said through clenched teeth.

"As you wish," he replied, as he pulled an AK from his coat.

In that exact moment, he pulled the trigger. As I attempted to duck for cover, several bullets hit me in the chest, and I went crashing into the wall behind me.

"Nooooooo," Judah screamed, and then came running into my direction but the bullets flying slowed him down.

Behind him, I saw someone creeping up, and I tried with all my might to warn him but no words escaped. Instead, I gurgled up blood, and my body grew weaker. Feeling completely helpless, I watched as Judah was smacked across the head with an AK 47. In slow motion, his body went crashing to the ground, and two men quickly grabbed him and dragged him behind the wall.

"No Judah, no Judah," I whispered, faintly.

Without my brothers I didn't know what I would do, or where I would be, and I don't even know if I could live. I almost didn't have the will to go on, but my brothers and the girls need me. Seeing that shit made me think back to

Sebastian; it wasn't like him to miss any important meetings, and he definitely would've been here for this. Knowing he wasn't here caused me to worry even more, and I could feel my soul trying to be ripped away. A lone tear escaped my heavy eyes as I fought with all my might to see through the fog. My only concern was Judah, as I tried to lift my head to see. Leaning over onto my side, I coughed blood onto the floor and repented for all my sins as my body grew lighter and lighter.

"Fuck, that damn Ava still fucking us over even in death," were the last words that escaped from me before the whole room went pitch black.

61313652R00123

Made in the USA
Lexington, KY
06 March 2017